A novelization by Jordan Horowitz
from a screenplay by Mark Saltzman
based on a screenplay by Simon Sheen

SCHOLASTIC INC.
New York Toronto London Auckland Sydney

TriStar Pictures presents a SHEEN production in association with BEN-AMI/LEEDS PRODUCTIONS a CHARLES T. KANGANIS film "3 NINJAS KICK BACK" VICTOR WONG MAX ELLIOTT SLADE SEAN FOX EVAN BONIFANT and SAB SHIMONO music by RICHARD MARVIN executive producers SIMON SHEEN YORAM BEN-AMI based on a screenplay by SIMON SHEEN PG PARENTAL GUIDANCE SUGGESTED screenplay by MARK SALTZMAN produced by JAMES KANG MARTHA CHANG ARTHUR LEEDS directed by CHARLES T. KANGANIS TRISTAR

Cover photo by Ron Slenzak.
Interior photos supplied by Youshiharu Nushida and Yoshiyaki Shina.

ISBN 0-590-48451-6

12 11 10 9 8 7 6 5   4 5 6 7 8 9/9

Printed in the U.S.A.   40

First Scholastic printing, May 1994

3 NINJAS KICK BACK

1.
Pursuit Through the Woods

The ninja warrior, dressed completely in black, darted from tree to tree. The three smaller ninja warriors had chased him through the forest and he was growing tired. Now he thought he had lost them. But when he looked up he saw the leering red mask of the first small warrior looking down at him.

He knew the warrior to be Rocky, so named because he was strong and solid.

Rocky leaped down from the branches of the tree and unleashed a series of quick kicks. The black-dressed ninja rolled away to avoid the kicks. In doing so he created a cloud of dust that camouflaged him as he ran farther off into the woods.

When the dust cleared it seemed as if he had disappeared into thin air.

They were good, these small warriors, the black-dressed ninja thought as he fled through the woods. They were very good.

1

He had come to the banks of a stream. He knew he had to cross the stream to escape his other two pursuers. But he had no sooner balanced himself upon a log and begun to cross when he heard something rustle in the trees above.

He looked up. Nothing. But when he looked back down, another small ninja was standing before him on the log. This one, who wore a blue mask, was the one named Colt, so called because he was fast and free, like the spirit of a young wild horse.

Colt had a *bo* stick and was twirling it at lightning speed. He inched his way toward the center of the log.

The black-dressed ninja spiraled around, fist extended, and knocked Colt off the log and into the stream. By the time Colt pulled himself back up onto the log, the black-dressed ninja had disappeared beyond some more trees.

They are swift and fast, thought the black-dressed ninja as he fled through the brush. I will be lucky to escape from them.

Suddenly, the black-dressed ninja had the feeling that he was being watched. He moved cautiously through the woods.

Then he heard it. The sound of a leaf being crushed by a small foot. He turned. From behind a bush came the third small warrior. The warrior wore a yellow mask with a mad grin painted across it. Dangling from that mad grin was a rubbery-looking piece of licorice.

The black-dressed ninja knew that he was face-to-face with the one named Tum Tum, so named because his energy began and ended with his tummy.

The black-dressed ninja acted quickly. He back-flipped, heels over hands, to avoid Tum Tum's attack. But when he regained his footing he saw that Tum Tum had been joined by the other two masked ninjas, Rocky and Colt. And all three were twirling *bo* sticks.

The black-dressed ninja picked up a thick fallen branch. Now the odds were even. The three small ninjas moved in, bunting at him with their *bo* sticks. He blocked each blow with short, precise turns. Then he felt the impact of Rocky's stick knock the branch from his hands.

The three ninjas hollered and charged. But the black-dressed ninja pulled a small pellet from his belt and hurled it to the ground. Upon impact the pellet exploded into a cloud of swirling smoke.

When the smoke cleared the black-dressed ninja was gone.

Tum Tum ripped the yellow mask from his face. "Why'd you get in my way, Colt?" he shouted accusingly through a missing baby tooth. He was only seven years old. "I had him!"

His brother Colt, eleven, removed his blue

mask. "You didn't get near him, Tum Tum," he replied.

"Did too," insisted Tum Tum. "Didn't I, Rocky?"

Rocky removed his red mask. At twelve he was the oldest of the three brothers and often had to be a referee when the other two argued. "Looks like Grandpa wins again," he sighed.

Just then the three boys heard someone laughing. They looked up. The black-dressed ninja was sitting in the limbs of a tree looking down at them. He removed his mask. Behind it was the smiling mustachioed face of Mori Shintaro, their grandfather.

His grandsons were right. He had, indeed, won again. But only barely. He had trained his grandchildren well. One more test and he would know if it was time to let them go.

2.
The Legend
of the Dagger

Mori brought the boys to a clearing in the woods where a practice dummy hung from the branch of a tree. He ordered them to line up and take turns kicking it.

"Remember, boys," he told them. "A true ninja is free of all desire. Only when you do not want can you be in control."

Tum Tum was first. "I don't want to kick him, I don't want to kick him, I don't want to kick him — " he repeated half aloud. Then he leaped up and took a stab at the dummy.

He missed.

"The more you want," began Mori, "the harder the task."

Colt and Rocky took their kick stances and tried next. But they missed, too.

"You have become sloppy," Mori told them. "Tum Tum, all the time eating. Colt, you have let your temper become your master. And Rocky, who knows where your head is?"

"I know!" said Tum Tum. "Lisa DiMarino! Lisa DiMarino!"

"Shut up!" Rocky ordered his baby brother. At the same time he knew Tum Tum was right. Lisa DiMarino was the prettiest girl in school and Rocky had a hard time thinking of anything but her.

"Remember," Mori said gently. "A ninja is heart, body, mind — "

"And spirit," finished Colt. And with that each boy took turns leaping forward and kicking.

BLINK! the dummy's eyes lit up as Tum Tum connected to its left shoulder.

BLINK! BLINK! Rocky hit the right shoulder.

BLINK! BLINK! BLINK! Colt smashed the bull's-eye, dead center in the chest.

When they were done Mori turned to them. "I have taught you all I know," he said proudly. "Now it is time for you to study with a teacher greater than myself."

They returned to Mori's cabin and changed into their regular clothes. As they did this Mori told them about the grand master of ninja who lived in Japan.

"Japan?" the boys shouted jumping up and down. "We're going to Japan?"

"Quiet! Quiet!" said Mori. "*I* must go there next

6

week, to my home town of Konang. I have arranged for you to come with me, to study with the grand master."

"All right! Grand master!" shouted Tum Tum excitedly, although he wasn't quite sure what a grand master was.

Mori removed a loose panel in the wall. There was a secret compartment hidden behind it.

"Wow," said Rocky. "I didn't even know that was there."

"That was the point," said Mori. He reached his arm into the compartment and pulled out a very old-looking dagger. The handle of the dagger was decorated with faded Japanese symbols. The boys crowded closer to see the dagger.

Mori told the boys of a time when he was just about their age, a young ninja living in Japan. One year he and another boy, Koga, were facing off in a ninja competition. The winner of the competition was to receive an ancient dagger.

There was a legend about the dagger and a *samurai* sword. When used together they could open the door to a cave of gold, laden with riches. Together they were like a key. Koga believed the legend and wanted to win the dagger badly.

But it was Mori who won the competition that year. The grand master presented him with the dagger.

After the ceremony was over, Koga attacked

Mori and tried to steal the dagger from him. But Mori was too quick. He swung around, ready to fight. During the fight Mori accidentally sliced Koga across the cheek with the dagger. Koga ran off. Mori had had the dagger ever since.

"What happened to that kid?" asked Colt when his grandfather had finished the story. "The one who wanted to steal your dagger?"

"Who knows?" replied Mori. "Just boys playing a long time ago. But now, *I* am the old master. I must take the dagger back and present it to the winner of the ninja tournament just as it was presented to me fifty years ago."

"What about the cave of gold?" asked Tum Tum. "Can we visit it when we go to Japan?"

"Weren't you listening, twerp," Colt said to his brother. "We need the sword to get in, too."

"Bigger twerp!" Tum Tum answered back.

"Biggest!" Colt retorted.

"Boys, boys, it was just a legend," Mori reminded them. "There is no cave of gold, and the sword — no one knows where it is."

But at that very moment, thousands of miles across the world in Japan, Koga stood before his mirror. He had put on his ceremonial ninja clothes and was looking at his face. It had aged greatly since that day many years ago when he lost the dagger to Mori Shintaro. He still had the scar across his cheek.

Koga knew that Mori still had the dagger. After all these years he would have the opportunity to steal it again. Once he had it, he would be able to find the cave of gold with all its riches.

But first he had to steal the sword. He knew exactly where it was and tonight it was going to be his.

He took one last look at the scar on his cheek. Then he covered his head with his ninja hood and climbed out through his window and into the night.

3.
The Sword

Koga moved from rooftop to rooftop, from shadow to shadow, until he reached the Japan Museum of History building on the hill. He stood on the roof of the building and looked down. When he saw that the street below was empty he unwound a rope from about his shoulder and tied it to a protruding pipeline.

Then he threw the rope over the side of the roof and began to inch his way down the side of the building. Within minutes he had snuck inside the museum and was making his way through its halls.

He stopped when he came upon the sign "Classic Samurai Swords." In the room ahead was what he was looking for. But he did not enter the room. Instead, he reached into a small pouch and sprinkled some baby powder onto the floor before him. The particles from the baby powder revealed a grid of razor thin red lights.

The alarm system.

Koga took a step back and then did a somersault over the beams. He landed inside the display room. Before him was a row of glass cases. In each case was a variety of *samurai* swords from different periods in Japanese history. Koga looked the swords over, searching, rejecting one dazzling artifact after another.

He finally came to a stop before one sword. Beneath the sword a small plaque read: "Ritual Samurai Sword from Konang." His mind flashed back to that day, fifty years earlier, when Mori had won the dagger that was the companion to the sword.

Tonight the sword would be his. He promised himself that in a few days the dagger would be his, too.

Koga reached into his pouch and pulled out a flat, disklike *shiruken* star. Its thin pointed edges were as sharp as knives. He used the edges to cut a hole in the glass case before him and then removed the sword.

The sword was now his. He returned to the entrance of the room and sprinkled some more powder over the floor and again leaped over the red beams.

Only this time the tip of the stolen sword sliced one of the beams. The alarm sounded through the halls of the museum.

Koga ran across the hall, turned down a stairway and found himself face-to-face with two security guards.

Koga whirled and landed two swift kicks into the guards. They went toppling down the stairs. Koga leaped over them and made his way upstairs to the roof exit.

He burst onto the roof. At the far end was a black winglike craft that he had placed there for his escape.

Koga headed for the glider when a shot rang out from behind him. He swerved around. One of the security guards had recovered on the stairway and chased Koga out onto the roof, his pistol drawn. Koga did a backflip and knocked the gun out of the guard's hand.

Then two more guards burst onto the roof and surrounded Koga. Koga twirled twice, legs bent, and sliced the guards down with two short, but swift ninja kicks. While the guards were on the floor of the roof writhing in pain, Koga rushed to the black craft, strapped himself in, and jumped off the side of the roof.

Koga dipped, but then the wind kicked in and pushed him up until he was gliding high over the Japanese city and on to freedom.

He returned to his elegant office and placed the sword on his desk. He studied its long, deadly shape. It was old and plain.

He took an envelope from his desk drawer and

opened it. He let two photographs slide out of the envelope and onto his desk.

One photograph was of the dagger and its intricately decorated handle.

The other photograph was of Mori Shintaro.

Koga held the photograph of Mori and looked at it closely. He could hardly wait to see his old enemy.

4.
Field of Battle

The baseball park was beginning to fill up. Kids from both teams, the Mustangs and the Dragons, were arriving with their parents. Rocky, Colt, and Tum Tum were dressed in their Dragons uniforms. Mori gathered them into a circle near the dugout.

"Before you go to Japan," began Mori, "you must be tested on this field of battle. Remember what I have taught you. Concentration, restraint, control. And unity. Four strands of rope. Separately they snap. Together, they are strong. Now, get out there."

Sam Douglas, the boys' father and Dragons coach, stood behind home plate. He didn't approve of their obsession with ninja ceremonies. He especially didn't like the fact that they now called themselves only by their ninja names.

"Mori!" Sam called out. "Leave the ninja stuff

for up at your cabin! Come on, guys! Let's take the field!"

The boys dropped their bags in the dugout. Then they took up positions on the baseball diamond. Colt was shortstop. Rocky stood on the pitcher's mound and threw warm-up balls to his dad.

"Keep it down, Samuel," directed his father. Then his dad looked around for Tum Tum. "Michael, where are you?" he called out.

Tum Tum, in full catcher's gear, was at the vendor's cart ordering two hot dogs. He wasn't called Tum Tum for nothing.

Mori sat next to Jessica Douglas in the bleachers. She was excited at seeing her children on the field.

"Don't they look adorable, dad?" she asked Mori. "My three little Hall of Famers."

"Yeah," smirked Mori. "The Monster Hall of Fame."

Just then a voice came over the loudspeaker and announced the start of the game.

Tum Tum took his position behind home plate, sneaking bites of his hot dogs through his catcher's mask. Rocky threw the first pitch to Keith, the Mustangs' batter. Keith popped the ball to home plate. Tum Tum threw his mask off to find the ball, causing his hot dog to go flying into the air.

He made a great catch — but it was the hot dog, not the ball.

Keith ran to first base. He looked over at second and saw that Colt was guarding the base. Then another Mustang batter hit the ball straight at Colt. Keith took off like lightning to second base and dipped in for a slide. But as he slid he aimed his spikes at Colt. Colt leaped out of Keith's way and bobbled the ball. Keith was safe at second.

Rocky wound up to throw the next pitch, but then someone caught his eye from the stands. It was Lisa DiMarino, the girl he liked most of all.

And she was smiling right at him!

Rocky's brain waves turned to mush. When he looked around at his teammates every member suddenly looked like Lisa DiMarino. And when he looked at the bleachers the entire crowd looked like hundreds of Lisa DiMarinos.

And all of them were chanting: "Rocky! Rocky! Rocky!"

He looked ahead at the batter: another Lisa DiMarino. Better throw an easy pitch, he thought. He wound up and let the ball go underhand.

The batter swung, hitting the ball with a CRACK!

Suddenly Rocky snapped back to reality. The batter wasn't Lisa DiMarino at all! It was a top

16

Mustangs player! The ball whizzed over his head and into the outfield.

By the time the Dragons got up to bat the Mustangs were ahead by two runs.

Colt was up first. He took some practice swings and waited for the ball. As he did this, the Mustangs' catcher made some horselike grunting sounds.

"Hey, Colt," teased the catcher. "Heard you get mad pretty easy. Gettin' mad now?" Then he made the horselike sounds again. "Gettin' mad, Colt?"

Colt started to push the catcher, but stopped when the umpire stepped in. Brushing himself off, he turned back to face the pitcher. The ball came and he swung.

And missed.

Colt tried to stay cool, but as he prepared for the next ball the catcher reached over and untied Colt's shoe. When Colt saw that his shoelace had become untied he took off his helmet and knelt down.

But while he tied his shoe, the catcher filled his helmet with dirt. Colt picked up his helmet and put it on. Dirt poured down his face.

"Ooops," laughed the catcher. "How'd that happen? Someone put dirt in your helmet? That's 'cause you're a dirt bag, Colt!"

At those words Colt dropped his bat and took

a ninja stance. He was ready to pounce on the catcher.

"Colt!" he heard a voice from the stands. It was Mori. "Control! Strength in restraint!"

He didn't want to, but Colt took a deep breath and relaxed his stance. Then he picked up his bat and faced the pitcher's mound. That's when he recognized the pitcher as Keith, the boy who had spiked him earlier.

Keith released a wild pitch, hitting Colt right on the helmet. POW! Colt landed in the dirt.

Colt had had enough. He got up, cracked his bat over his knee and lunged at Keith, using the bat pieces as two ninja sticks. But as he did so the catcher made a dive for Colt's ankles and wrestled him to the ground.

Before long the rest of the players from both teams rushed in and joined the fight. Soon the whole baseball diamond was crowded with fighting, howling kids. Parents descended from the stands and tried to break up the fight.

When the brawl was over the umpire lined up both teams on the baseball field and reprimanded them. As punishment, he suspended the game for a week.

"How can we replay the game next Sunday?" complained Tum Tum as he and his brothers loaded their baseball gear into their father's car thirty minutes later. "We'll be in Japan with Grandpa."

"We're not going to Japan," replied Colt. "We're going to play baseball."

"What are you talking about?" asked Rocky.

"I wanna go!" shouted Tum Tum.

"I wanna play!" shouted Colt.

Suddenly Sam Douglas slammed down the hood of the trunk. "I want! I want!" he mimicked his sons. "What's the matter with you? You call yourselves a team out there? You embarrassed yourselves and you made me ashamed."

"How can I pay attention with Grandpa pestering me from the stands like that?" asked Colt. *"That's* what's embarrassing."

"Rocky," continued Sam. "What were you looking at when you were supposed to be pitching? And Colt, you fighting like that. I've told you about that temper! You've got to learn to control it!"

Sam turned to Mori, who was listening with Jessica at the side of the car. "You see what this ninja stuff does?" Sam told his father-in-law. "All they want to do is fight."

"Does this mean no Japan?" asked Tum Tum.

"It may mean no to a lot of things," threatened Sam. "Until you all decide to grow up."

Sam locked the trunk and motioned for everyone to get into the car. Inside, Jessica could see that Mori was heartbroken that the boys might not be allowed to journey to Japan with him.

"Four strands," Mori sighed half aloud. "I think our rope is beginning to unravel."

As the car pulled out of the parking lot, Mori turned to look at the boys. They turned their heads, ashamed to look their grandfather in the face.

5.
Assignment: Dagger

The heavy metal band was playing its heart out. The leader, white-haired Glam, was on bass. Slam banged the drums and Vinnie wailed on lead guitar.

It was audition night at the club and they wanted to make a good impression for the club manager. So they wore their grungiest clothes and played extra loud.

"Stop!" shouted the manager. "Pull the plug!"

The band abruptly stopped playing.

"Listen, you guys," the manager continued. "Let me give you some career advice. You stink. Anything you don't understand about that? The 'you' part? The 'stink' part? Glam, you get behind the bar, do the job you were hired for. The rest of you, get out of my club."

"I told you we should have rehearsed," Glam told the others as they packed up their instruments.

"Oh, yeah," remembered the manager. "Glam, there's a phone call for you."

Glam went behind the bar, brushed his stark-white, shoulder-length hair behind his ears, and picked up the phone. It was his uncle Koga, calling all the way from Japan. He had sent Glam an overnight envelope and wanted to know if it had been received. Glam reached down and pulled the envelope out from behind the bar. Then he opened it. Inside were two photographs. One was of Mori. The other was of the dagger.

"Cool knife," Glam commented. Then he listened carefully as Koga instructed him to find Mori and steal the knife.

"I will pay you well to perform this task for me," Koga concluded.

Glam agreed. Then he gathered Slam and Vinnie, stuffed the photos into his leather coat, and left the club.

Rocky, Colt, and Tum Tum were spending their last day at the cabin. Tum Tum was slicing up a salad with a ninja sword. Rocky was trying to translate a soup recipe from a Japanese cookbook. Colt was off in a corner playing cards by himself. He was sulking because he and his brothers had blown the baseball championship and, quite possibly, their trip to Japan.

Mori was on the telephone ordering airplane tickets to Japan.

"How many tickets?" Mori repeated to the ticket agent on the other end of the line. "I'm not sure . . ."

"Get one for me!" shouted Tum Tum. Then he swacked another tomato with his sword.

"No!" Colt cut in.

"You must decide now," said Mori. "I have to tell the travel agent."

"It's *Japan*, Colt," Rocky told his brother. "How often do we get a chance like this? You want to throw it away?"

"What about winning the baseball championship?" Colt retorted. "You want to throw that away?"

"I want to go," said Tum Tum.

"Your vote doesn't count," Colt said to his baby brother.

"It does too!" exclaimed Tum Tum.

"Rocky," began Colt. "You could pitch the winning game. What do you think Lisa DiMarino would think of that?"

Rocky agreed with Colt.

"We voted," Colt said, turning to Mori. "We're going to play baseball."

"All right," Mori said sadly. So he ordered just one ticket for himself. Then he put on his hat, got into his car, and drove off to pick up his airplane ticket.

As Mori turned onto the main highway, an old pickup truck pulling a camper passed him from the other direction. Inside were Glam, Slam, and Vinnie.

"I think that's him!" said Glam, pointing to Mori's car. He held up the photos of Mori and the dagger.

Slam grabbed the picture of the dagger. "No wonder your uncle's paying us twenty grand," he said. "That's a nice letter opener!"

"He's gone," said Vinnie as he watched Mori drive off in his rearview mirror. "That means the cabin's empty."

"Rock and roll!!!" shouted Slam and Vinnie eagerly. They picked up speed and headed for the cabin.

In the cabin, Rocky and Tum Tum turned to Colt as they cleaned up the mess they had made in the kitchen.

"You're really being a jerk to Grandpa," Rocky said to Colt.

"Me?" replied Colt. "You wanted to stay, too."

"Sometimes I think you don't even *want* to be a ninja anymore," added Tum Tum accusingly.

"I never said that!" insisted Colt.

Suddenly an alarm sounded. The boys looked over to a ninja mask that hung above the door. It was buzzing to life with flashing lights.

"Somebody's coming!" exclaimed Rocky.

"Robbers," said Colt.

"Or maybe somebody's lost," said Tum Tum.

"Ninjas should always be prepared for battle," Rocky reminded his brothers. "Or to give directions."

The boys scrambled to the window and peeked out. Outside they saw Glam, Slam, and Vinnie climb out of their pickup truck.

"As long as we're in there," they heard Vinnie suggest, "let's steal any hardware: CD players, speakers, TV . . ."

"Slammin'!" agreed Slam. Then the three of them headed straight for the cabin.

Rocky, Colt, and Tum Tum looked at each other. They knew what they had to do. They ran into their attic bedroom and switched into their ninja uniforms.

Colt hid in the bedroom while Tum Tum went into the kitchen and loaded up on some ammo: eggs, pie, a can of soda, and a container of whipped cream. Then he went into the pantry and waited.

Rocky grabbed a spool of fishing wire and climbed out of a back window. He snuck around the side of the cabin and tied one end of the fishing wire to the knob of the front door. Then he took the other end and climbed up a nearby tree.

Outside, Glam took his position as lookout. Slam

and Vinnie approached the cabin with a crowbar. But just as they reached the front door, Rocky yanked the fishing wire tightly. The door jerked open suddenly and Slam and Vinnie tumbled, one on top of the other, into the cabin.

"Owww! Get offa me!" ordered Vinnie.

Slam rose to his feet. He noticed a desk in the corner.

"Hey, look!" Slam said, pointing. "A desk!"

"So?" asked Vinnie.

"If you were going to hide a letter opener, wouldn't you put it there?"

Slam went to the desk and opened the drawers. He pulled out a plain metal letter opener.

"I found it!" he said. "Let's go."

"Were you hatched from a moron egg?" Vinnie asked Slam. He held out the photo of the dagger with its decorated handle. "Does *that* look like *this*? I'll go upstairs."

Vinnie began climbing the stairs to the attic bedroom. Meanwhile Slam nosed around the kitchen. He decided that the pantry was a likely place to hide a dagger. He tried opening the pantry door, but it was stuck. He tried again. This time the door flew open and Slam was hit square in the face by a stream of soda spray. Then the door slammed itself shut.

Slam opened the pantry door again. This time

a dozen eggs, rapid fire, pelted him in the face. Then the door closed itself again.

Now Slam was angry. He yanked the door open a third time. This time he was rammed in the stomach by Tum Tum, the human missile. Tum Tum scissor-kicked Slam in the stomach and sent him flying across the room into a bookcase.

"Hey, Vinnie!" called Slam. "The house ain't empty!"

"What are you talking about?" shouted Vinnie from the attic bedroom. He looked all over and couldn't see anybody. "There's nobody here!"

Just then something stirred on one of the beds.

"KEIIIII!" came a scream. It was Colt, who exploded from under a blanket and landed a kick into Vinnie's chest. Vinnie went tumbling down the attic stairs. He landed right on top of Slam, knocking both of them to the ground.

Outside, Glam was getting bored. He pulled out a microphone from his pocket and pretended he was giving the rock and roll concert of the decade.

That's when he was hit on the head with a pinecone. Glam looked up at a tree.

"Hey," he called out. "Who's up there?" He grabbed a stick and moved around the tree.

"Up here, grunge-breath," came Rocky's voice from high in the tree. Glam looked up. Suddenly Rocky let fly with a dozen more pinecones. Each one hit Glam on the head. Glam screamed and ran toward the cabin.

Inside the cabin, while Vinnie and Slam struggled to their feet, Colt and Tum Tum poured cooking oil on the floor. When they were out of oil they added a trail of whipped cream.

Vinnie and Slam saw Colt and Tum Tum across the room, standing at the front door.

"Oh, please, Mr. Man," taunted Tum Tum. "Don't hurt us!"

Vinnie and Slam lunged forward toward the boys. Suddenly they started sliding on the oil and whipped cream. With flailing arms they sailed across the floor. At the last possible moment the boys parted to each side and Colt opened the front door.

WHAM! Vinnie and Slam smashed into Glam, who was just making his way up the front porch. All three hoodlums went falling to the ground.

"Who are you guys?" asked Glam as soon as he could see clearly. "The Midget Mutants?"

"Not!" shouted Rocky as he climbed down from the tree and joined his two brothers on the porch. "We're the three ninjas!"

"Let's get out of here while we're still standing," said Slam. Then he and Vinnie started back toward the van.

But Glam decided to challenge the three ninjas. He ran off around the side of the cabin. Rocky,

Colt, and Tum Tum followed. Glam sneaked around the house and came around from the other side. Then he ran in the front door.

Glam studied the cabin. "If I were a dagger," he muttered to himself, "where would I hide?"

Glam noticed a shiny object on the floor near the wrecked bookcase. He took a step forward, but as he did so he slid on a trail of whipped cream and fell flat on his face. After a moment he opened his eyes. The shiny object was within arm's reach.

And it was the dagger. It had fallen out of the secret compartment during the fight.

The three ninjas were about to follow Glam into the cabin when they heard the sudden sound of the van's ignition. Rocky and Colt grabbed a rope. Rocky tied one end around the van's towing hitch while Colt pulled the other end into the cabin.

Colt saw that Glam was on the floor reaching for the dagger. He quickly tied his end of the rope around Glam's ankles.

At the same time, Slam shifted the van into drive and hit the gas pedal with his foot. The vehicle peeled away.

Inside the cabin, Glam was about to tighten his fingers around the dagger when he felt a slight tug at his feet. He looked down and saw the rope around his ankles. The rope contracted and yanked him away from the dagger. Next he was pulled across the floor, out the front door of the house, and across the yard. It wasn't until he felt himself being dragged straight across the bridge and toward the main road that he realized one of the boys had tied him to the back of the van.

"Come and see us again!" Colt shouted from the front porch of the cabin. He, Rocky, and Tum Tum doubled over laughing as they watched the hoodlums disappear into the distance.

The three ninjas had saved the day.

6.
Incident in Tokyo

The following morning Rocky, Colt, and Tum Tum watched as Mori packed his suitcase. In a few hours their grandfather would be on his way to Japan.

After breakfast the boys heard their parents' car pull up outside. They were going to drive Mori to the airport before taking the boys home.

"I think dad is really disappointed that the boys aren't going to Japan with him," Jessica said as she helped Sam load suitcases into the car.

"Everything they need to know about life they can learn on the baseball field, the way I did," said Sam. "It'll be good for them to be away from this ninja stuff for a while."

The boys were watching from the front porch and heard every word. Jessica walked over to them.

"Don't forget," she reminded them. "Your dad was a kid once, too."

"No way," growled Colt with resentment. "He was born full grown, with a suitcase."

Sam locked the trunk and motioned for everyone to get into the car.

"Aaah!" exclaimed Mori with a snap of his fingers. "I almost forgot the most important thing."

He ran back into the cabin. A moment later he returned holding the dagger. He displayed it proudly to Jessica and Sam before packing it into his ninja bag.

Glam, Slam, and Vinnie were hidden behind some trees. They watched as the Douglas family drove away. When they saw that Mori had taken the dagger with him, they climbed into their van and followed him to the airport.

At the airport the hoodlums watched from a distance as Sam helped Mori unload his luggage.

"Which one of these bags is yours, Mori?" asked Sam.

"The one with no sticker," answered Mori.

Sam looked through the trunk of the car, pulled out a ninja bag, and handed it to Mori. Mori turned to face the boys.

"Good-bye, boys," he said sadly. "I wish you were coming with me."

Tum Tum ran forward and gave Mori a big hug. "Me, too, Grandpa," he said.

Colt and Rocky looked at each other. They felt too guilty to even say good-bye to Mori.

The Douglas family piled back into their car and drove off. Mori waved good-bye one last time, then turned and walked through the automatic doors of the airport terminal.

"Hey, there he goes with the bag!" observed Glam. He and his partners were across the lane watching from their van.

"Where's who going?" asked Slam.

"I don't know," said Vinnie. "But we're going, too."

"Where's *who* going?" Slam asked again.

"The guy with the bag," answered Vinnie.

"Where?" asked Slam.

"I don't know," answered Vinnie.

All three looked at each other. "Vacation time!!!" they shouted in unison. It was clear that Mori was going *somewhere*. The only way the grungers were going to find out *where* was by going there, too.

Glam, Slam, and Vinnie followed Mori into the terminal. They saw him get on an airplane going to Japan. So they bought three tickets and boarded the same plane.

Fifteen hours later the plane landed at Tokyo airport. Mori hailed a taxi cab, stuffed his ninja bag into the trunk, and told the driver to take him to his hotel. Glam, Slam, and Vinnie followed in a rented van.

33

The streets of Tokyo were crowded with people and cars. Traffic moved very slowly. Mori smiled as he looked through the taxi cab window. Although he now lived with his family in the U.S., Japan would always be his home.

The traffic light changed to red and the taxi came to a stop. A few cars behind, Slam slowed the van to a stop as well. Seeing the opportunity to steal Mori's ninja bag, Vinnie and Glam got out of the van. They weaved their way through the waiting cars until they reached the taxi. But before they could pry open the trunk, the light turned green and the taxi pulled out.

Vinnie and Glam raced back to their van and climbed in. Slam hit the gas and followed after the taxi. He swerved in and around the cars ahead of him until he was right behind the taxi.

Suddenly the traffic light turned red again. SKREECH! CRASH! The van smashed into the back of the taxi causing the trunk to pop open.

Now Mori's ninja bag was in clear view.

Vinnie and Glam jumped out of the van and grabbed the bag. Seeing this through the rear window, Mori bounded out of the taxi and marched toward the thieves.

Just then the traffic light turned to green and Mori heard a noise from behind. He turned to see a car bearing down on him at top speed.

Mori leaped out of the way of the oncoming car,

but it was too late. The force of the impact rolled him over the car's hood and onto the concrete sidewalk.

Mori tried to get up, but couldn't. Through his barely conscious eyes he could see Vinnie and Glam hustle his ninja bag into their van and drive off.

It was the last thing he saw before losing consciousness.

7.
Who's Holding the Bag?

Koga looked down at the mileage counter on the treadmill. He had already run the equivalent of nine miles. Just one more mile and he would reach his daily goal. Around him was his office. A huge window overlooked the Tokyo countryside. On a hill in the distance was an old castle.

Standing at his side was his bodyguard, Ishikawa. Ishikawa was a giant-sized man. He held a tray with water and a towel for Koga's cooldown. His loyalty to Koga was complete. As long as he was alive no one would harm Koga.

Just then the office door burst open. Glam, Slam, and Vinnie tumbled in, nearly tripping over each other. Vinnie held Mori's ninja bag.

"Greetings, Uncle!" Glam said to Koga.

Koga continued to work the treadmill, his concentration uninterrupted by the intrusion.

"I was expecting you earlier," said Koga.

"We did your bidding," added Glam. "And we got the goods right here."

Koga continued his workout. Although he had been eagerly awaiting the arrival of his nephew, he showed no excitement. Then, when the treadmill meter clicked ten miles, Koga stepped off the machine. Ishikawa presented his master with the tray. Koga dampened the towel and began to wipe the sweat from his face.

"I don't know if you know this," Slam said to Koga. "But everybody in your country drives on the wrong side. I was turning this corner, you know and — "

"Quiet, fool," Koga said, cutting Slam off. He returned the towel to the tray. "Give it to me."

"Behold, Uncle!" announced Glam. "The dagger of doom!"

Glam nodded to Vinnie. Vinnie unzipped the ninja bag and stuck his hand inside.

Then he screamed.

He yanked his hand out. There was a mousetrap clamped to his fingers.

Koga grabbed the bag and dumped the contents out onto his desk. There were bags of licorice, jelly beans, jumbo candy bars, and beef jerky sticks. There was also a little boy's ninja uniform.

Glam and the others were stunned. This wasn't Mori's bag at all.

"You have failed me again," Koga grumbled to Glam and the others.

"Uncle, I can explain — !" begged Glam.

Koga turned to his giant servant. "Ishikawa," he commanded. "Show them how we handle fools."

Ishikawa swiftly grabbed Glam and tied him to the treadmill. Then he turned the treadmill on at top speed. Glam screamed as his feet tried to keep up with the machine.

"Nephew," said Koga. "I am much dissatisfied."

"Yes," whimpered Glam. "I'm sorry, Uncle."

"But I am prepared to give you another chance," Koga continued. "Mori Shintaro is in Japan?"

"Yes," Glam said breathlessly. His feet were getting tired. "We followed him here!"

"Keep watching him," ordered Koga. "Listen to his every word. Find out where that dagger is and bring it to me."

"Yes! Yes, my dearest uncle!" said Glam. "My favorite relative!"

Koga nodded to Ishikawa. Ishikawa turned the treadmill off. Glam jerked forward and hit his head on the treadmill handlebars.

Slam and Vinnie looked at each other. They were terrified of Koga.

"And that's his *favorite* uncle," whispered Slam.

Glam, Slam, and Vinnie left Koga's office, bowing humbly as they did. After they were gone, Koga looked down at the ninja bag on his desk and scowled at its childish contents.

If this wasn't Mori's bag, he wondered, then whose was it?

8.
A Message from Grandpa

The telephone was ringing just as Tum Tum, Rocky, and Colt got home from school. Rocky raced to the phone and answered it, but not before the answering machine beeped and began recording.

It was Mori calling from Japan. And he didn't sound happy.

"Boys, I'm all right," he told his grandsons. The three boys huddled around the receiver. "But I'm in the hospital in Tokyo. I'm fine. Ouch! Not so hard, nurse!"

Mori was propped up in a hospital bed while Nurse Hino, who looked like a sumo wrestler, was tightening a pressure band around Mori's arm and taking his blood pressure.

"What's wrong, Grandpa?" asked Colt worriedly.

"Nothing much," replied Mori. "I was in a tiny car accident — just a few bruises. But I'm at the

40

mercy of an ugly witch posing as a nurse."

Nurse Hino squeezed the pressure band tighter.

"OUCH! Leave me alone, I'm talking to my grandsons!" Mori scolded the nurse. "OUCH! Easy, you vampire!

"I'm okay," Mori assured his grandsons. "But my luggage got stolen by a weird-looking Asian guy with long white hair. Yes, all of it. Even the dagger."

"They stole the dagger!" Rocky said to his brothers.

"Just don't tell your parents about this," continued Mori. "I don't want to worry them. I just wanted you to know."

"We won't tell Mom and Dad," promised Rocky.

"I'm in Tokyo General," said Mori. "A fine hospital. Except for this wicked nurse, with a face like a dragon."

"Okay, Grandpa," said Rocky. "I hope you feel better. Bye-bye."

Rocky hung up the phone.

"Did he say who hit him?" asked Colt.

"Some Asian guy with white hair," explained Rocky.

"Like that jerko metalhead that tried to rob the cabin?" asked Tum Tum. He had just returned from the kitchen and was stuffing a cream-filled chocolate cake into his mouth.

Suddenly it dawned on the boys. The metal-heads that attacked them at the cabin had followed Mori to Japan!

Tum Tum finished his cake, but was still hungry. He opened his ninja bag and looked for a stick of beef jerky. But when he looked inside all he could find was Mori's dagger.

The three ninjas stared at the dagger. They realized that Mori must have taken Tum Tum's bag to Japan by mistake.

"Grandpa's in trouble," said Rocky. "Those guys are after his dagger."

"We gotta go there," said Colt. "Right away. We gotta help him."

"But Colt," began Rocky. "What about the baseball game?"

"That's just a game," replied Colt. "This is Grandpa. Blood is thicker than Gatorade."

"We got a lot to do," said Rocky. "First, I'll take care of the tickets."

Rocky turned Mori's bag upside down and dumped its contents out on a table. Then he rummaged through them until he found Mori's credit card.

"You're going to use that?" asked Colt.

"He'd want us to," replied Rocky.

Rocky looked up the number for a travel agent and dialed the phone. He ordered three tickets to Japan.

"So that's three children's fares to Tokyo?" asked the ticket agent on the other end of the line.

"We're almost grown-up," insisted Rocky.

"And the name on the card?" asked the ticket agent.

"Mori Shintaro," answered Rocky. "He's my grandfather."

"I'm afraid we'll need his authorization," explained the ticket agent. "Can I talk to him?"

Rocky hesitated. He needed a way to trick the ticket agent into thinking Mori was buying the tickets. Then he noticed the answering machine and got an idea.

"Is Grandpa's message still on the tape from the answering machine?" Rocky whispered to Colt.

Colt nodded and brought the machine over to the telephone. Then he rewound the tape.

"*Hello?*" came Mori's voice from the answering machine.

"Mr. Shintaro?" asked the ticket agent. He thought Mori was really talking to him! "How are you today?"

Colt quickly pressed a switch on the answering machine. The tape sped forward.

"*I'm fine,*" came Mori's voice.

"That's nice," said the ticket agent. "I just took a reservation on your card by a young man — "

Colt fast forwarded the tape again. "*My grandson,*" said Mori's voice. Colt and Rocky gave each

43

other a thumbs-up. By using some of the words from their conversation with their grandfather they had convinced the ticket agent that Mori was actually on the phone. They continued to press the fast forward and reverse buttons on the answering machine.

"Three seats this afternoon to — " continued the ticket agent.

" — *Tokyo* — "

"So I have your authorization?"

"Ouch! Not so hard!"

Colt suddenly stopped the tape. It wasn't easy finding the right phrases.

"I'm sorry?" asked the travel agent. "Is this amount okay with you?"

Colt pressed the play button again. *"Yes. All of it — "* came Mori's voice. Then the tape jumped again. *"You vampire!"*

The travel agent was taken aback. "Really, sir," he retorted. "I don't set the prices, I just work here. I'll run this through. Your grandsons can pick up the tickets at the airport. Have a nice day."

Colt pressed the play button. *"Ugly old witch!"* exclaimed Mori's voice.

"Oh, yeah?" replied the travel agent. "Well, you know what you are? You're a — "

Rocky moved the receiver away from the answering machine. "Good-bye!" he told the travel agent and immediately hung up.

"Okay," said Rocky turning to his brothers. "We gotta get it in gear. I'll write a note to Mom and Dad. Colt, you find all the money in the house. Tum Tum, you call a cab. We'll be packed by the time it gets here."

"How we gonna do all that before Mom and Dad get home?" asked Tum Tum.

"You've heard of ingenuity?" replied Rocky. "This is ninja-nuity. Let's go!"

The three boys scrambled like lightning. Colt smashed his piggy bank and filled his ninja bag with coins. Tum Tum called a taxi service and ordered a car to take them to Los Angeles Airport. Then he emptied a drawer full of candy into his ninja bag. Rocky scribbled a note to his parents and posted it on the stair banister.

By the time they had finished all their packing the doorbell rang. It was the taxi.

"Shuttle!" announced Colt. The three brothers carried their bags to the front door.

Tum Tum hesitated. "But I don't want to leave Mom and Dad," he whined.

"Come on, Tum Tum," said Rocky. "This is for Grandpa!"

Tum Tum sighed with resignation. Then he took a photo of Sam and Jessica from the breakfront and stuffed it into his pocket. Having the photo with him made him feel better. He followed his brothers out of the house and into the waiting taxi. In a few minutes they would be on their way to Japan.

9.
Nurses
and Ninjas

After landing at Tokyo Airport, Rocky, Colt, and Tum Tum began looking for a taxi. The main terminal was a mad rush of people and the boys felt overwhelmed by the bustle.

"Let's just stick together," said Rocky. "Let's get a taxi."

Just then the boys heard some screams. They looked over to see a well-dressed Japanese woman struggling with a thief. The thief yanked the woman's handbag from her hand and started running away.

Thinking quickly, Colt unzipped his ninja bag, pulled out a baseball, and tossed it to Rocky. Rocky aimed the ball, wound up, and pitched it toward the fleeing robber.

BONK! The baseball conked the robber on the back of the head and knocked him to the ground.

The boys ran after the robber. When he saw them coming the thief dropped the purse and fled.

Tum Tum retrieved the handbag. He and his brothers carried it back to the woman, who was waiting next to her limousine and chauffeur. The woman was very grateful and thanked them in Japanese. They had no idea what she was saying.

"She says thank-you," translated the chauffeur. Although he was also Japanese, he spoke some English. "She wants to repay you."

The boys smiled at each other.

"Could you give us a ride?" asked Tum Tum. "To Tokyo General Hospital?"

The chauffeur and the woman discussed something in Japanese.

"She wants to know," began the chauffeur. "Are you sick?"

"No, we're fine," explained Rocky. "But our grandfather's there."

"Mori Shintaro," added Tum Tum. "Do you know him?"

"No," answered the chauffeur. "But it will be our pleasure to take you to him."

The boys piled into the back of the limousine. There was plenty of room. There was also a refrigerator and a TV. The woman opened the refrigerator. It was filled with food. Tum Tum's eyes widened.

The woman said something to the chauffeur, who had slid behind the steering wheel of the limo.

"She asked if you would like something to eat?" translated the chauffeur.

"Well, if you insist," agreed Tum Tum. "What is it?"

The woman pulled out a plate of raw fish.

"Sashimi, a Japanese delicacy," replied the chauffeur. "Raw fish."

Rocky and Colt made faces and groaned at the idea of eating raw fish. But Tum Tum just shrugged. He grabbed the raw fish and scarfed it down.

After all, food was food.

Thirty minutes later the limousine arrived at Tokyo General Hospital. The boys thanked the woman and the chauffeur for the ride and entered the hospital. Tum Tum grabbed one last piece of sashimi and followed his brothers.

They found Mori's room on the third floor. As they approached the door they heard their grandfather let out a loud scream. They rushed into the room to find Mori laying on his side. Nurse Hino had just finished giving him an injection.

"Can't you be a little bit gentle?" Mori asked the nurse.

"Really, Mr. Shintaro," said Nurse Hino. "My grandchildren behave better than you do."

"Well, *my* grandchildren would drive you out of town with a ninja stick for that," Mori snapped back as he rubbed his backside. "Owww . . ."

"He's right," said Tum Tum. "We would!"

Mori and Nurse Hino turned around to see Tum Tum and the others standing at the foot of the bed.

"Boys!" exclaimed Mori with surprise. "What are you doing here?"

The boys rushed forward and embraced their grandfather.

"I'm very glad to see you," smiled Mori. "Nurse Hino, these are my three ninjas. Come back later."

Nurse Hino smiled at the boys and left the room.

"We think you're in a lot of danger, Grandpa," said Colt once Nurse Hino had left the room.

"Danger? What danger?"

Just then the door opened and an orderly quietly slipped into the room with a pill cart. The orderly wore a surgical cap and mask. From under the cap jutted out whisps of white hair.

It was Glam. But the boys didn't notice him through his disguise.

"The guy you said stole your luggage," Rocky began to explain to Mori. "The Asian guy with the white hair?"

"He's the same guy who tried to rob the cabin," added Colt.

Glam tried not to react to the conversation. Instead, he pulled a small microphone from under the cart and placed it, unseen, on the night table next to Mori's bed.

"How do you know all that?" Mori asked the boys.

"Did he look like a kind of heavy metal chump?" asked Rocky.

"Like he was trying to be a grunge rock star?" asked Colt.

"But just came off like a major drip?" asked Rocky.

Glam winced. The boys were describing him! He took some empty medicine vials from Mori's night table, orderly-style, and left the room.

Outside Glam tossed his orderly costume into a trash can and left the hospital. He joined Slam and Vinnie in their van. They were parked right under Mori's room. The van was now filled with all kinds of specialized surveillance equipment like microphones and recording devices. Now that Glam had put a microphone near Mori's bed, the hoodlums could hear every word that was being said.

"We think those guys were after the dagger, Grandpa," they heard Colt say.

"Well, they have it now," replied Mori.

Inside Mori's room Rocky pulled the dagger out of his bag.

"Rocky! How?" asked Mori.

"You took Tum Tum's bag by mistake," explained Rocky.

"And they got my Ding Dongs!" added Tum Tum sadly.

Glam, Slam, and Vinnie looked at each other inside the van. "Did you hear that?" asked Vinnie. "Those kids got it!"

"Got what?" asked Slam.

"The dagger!" answered Glam.

Back in his hospital room, Mori smiled at his grandsons with pride. "So you came all this way to Japan because you thought I was in trouble?" he asked. "What did you tell your parents?"

"Well, we, uh — " mumbled Rocky.

"We left them a note," said Colt.

"Oh, no," said Mori. He immediately picked up the telephone and dialed the boys' home number. Jessica answered. "Hello, Jessica? Yes. How are you? How's the weather there? The boys? Oh, let me see . . . oh, yes, they *are* here. Just a second."

Mori held the phone straight out.

"Hi, Mom!!" the boys shouted into the receiver.

"Now it's not their fault," Mori told Jessica. He wanted to get the boys off the hook. "I told them to come. I missed them. They'll be fine. Talk to Tum Tum."

Tum Tum took the receiver. "Hi, Mom," he said.

Jessica was so relieved that her children were

safe and sound that she did not even yell at Tum Tum. Instead, she told him to set the beeper on his watch and call her every day at 2 PM.

After Tum Tum had set his watch everyone said good-bye and hung up the phone.

Now it was time to deal with the matter at hand.

"The tournament is going on in Konang now," Mori told them. "You boys take the dagger there for me, and present it to the winner of the competition."

"But what about you, Grandpa?" asked Colt.

"They're releasing me from the hospital in a few days," explained Mori. "I'll meet you there then."

Just then Nurse Hino came back in. She was wearing a wicked smile and holding the syringe.

"Didn't I tell you to go away?" said Mori.

"Do you know how I deal with troublesome patients?" asked Nurse Hino. And with that she let out a loud bark and did a series of karate chops into the air. The boys jumped out of her way. "Now roll over!" she ordered.

"I'll make a deal," offered Mori. "I'll let you use me as a pincushion if you see to it that my boys get on the train to Konang."

"I'll be glad to help," agreed Nurse Hino. "I have grandchildren of my own. This is the end of my shift, anyway."

"Thank goodness," muttered Mori.

"Nurse Shabuya will be taking my place."

The door opened and Nurse Shabuya entered the room.

Mori and the boys swallowed hard when they saw her. She was twice as big as Nurse Hino.

Nurse Shabuya took the syringe from Nurse Hino and leaned toward Mori with a menacing smile.

The boys could only cover their eyes and wince at what was coming next.

10.
Some Time to Kill

When Nurse Hino was given a job to do she took it very seriously. That was why she was such a good nurse. Now her job was to see that Mori Shintaro's grandchildren were given safe passage to the *dojo*, the martial arts school in Konang where the ninja tournament would be taking place.

The first thing she did was place the boys in single file. Then she marched them, army-style, out of the hospital.

Outside the hospital, Glam, Slam, and Vinnie watched from their van as Nurse Hino led the boys away. The boys were carrying their ninja bags. The hoodlums knew that in one of them was the dagger.

Slam gently stepped on the gas and pulled the van out. He followed slowly behind Nurse Hino and the boys. He trailed them until they arrived at the train station. Then he and his partners got out of the van and followed on foot.

There were thirty minutes left before the train for Konang would be leaving. The boys looked around for something to do. Luckily, the lobby of the train station was filled with all kinds of shops. Among the shops was a video parlor.

Score! Rocky, Colt, and Tum Tum loved video games. They went inside and started playing. They were happy to see some of their favorite games in the arcade. There were also some games they had never seen before.

One of the new games was called *pachinko*. It reminded Colt of an old-style pinball machine. He pulled a lever and a tiny ball shot up through the machine, scoring points as it went. When he scored enough points a bunch of balls would slide down an open chute.

Colt was good at *pachinko*. He scored over and over again. And with each score more balls collected in the slot.

Glam, Slam, and Vinnie were hiding behind some video game machines. They were watching Colt. His ninja bag was draped around his shoulder. They carefully came out from behind the machines and slinked their way toward the bag.

Colt was too busy concentrating on the game

to see the three metalheads sneaking up behind him. He scored again. Then again and again. Soon the open chute overflowed with *pachinko* balls. The balls tumbled out and spilled onto the floor.

The balls scattered across the parlor floor just as Vinnie was about to swipe Colt's ninja bag. Vinnie slipped on the balls and fell backwards, right into Slam and Glam. The three hoodlums tumbled back like dominoes.

Just then Nurse Hino stepped into the parlor. She grabbed Colt by the ear and pulled him away from the *pachinko* game.

The train to Konang was about to leave.

Nurse Hino and Colt joined Rocky and Tum Tum on the train platform. Not far behind, Vinnie, Slam, and Glam hid behind a luggage cart. As soon as the three ninjas boarded the train Glam gave a signal to his partners. Then the three of them rushed out toward the train — and right into Nurse Hino.

THUD! The three scruffs bounced off Nurse Hino and landed on the ground.

"Get out of our way!" Glam ordered Nurse Hino. He and the others got up and tried to move around the giant nurse. But she blocked them with a karate stance. Then she let out a loud karate yell and administered three quick chops to their necks and shoulders. They fell to the ground like dead weight.

By the time they were able to get back on their feet the train had pulled out. The boys, with the dagger, were gone.

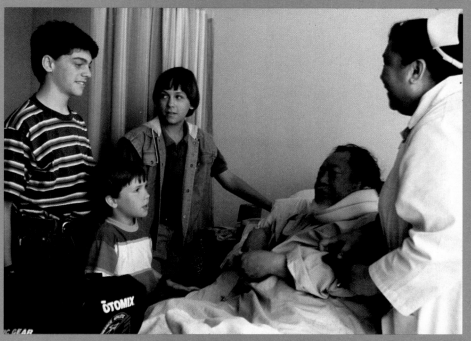

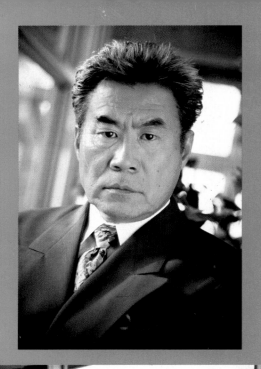

11.
The Dojo

Rocky, Colt, and Tum Tum got out of the cab and stood in front of the *dojo*, the martial arts school in Konang. It was here, in the school's gymnasium, that the ninja tournament was about to begin.

The three boys entered the gymnasium and took their seats in the bleachers. The gym was a rainbow of team costumes and banners. The bleachers were filled with parents, watching their kids doing martial arts warm-ups. The parents yelled out to their kids on the gym floor. Others were arguing with the referees. Some also had video cameras.

There was even a fast food vendor climbing the bleachers selling chicken *yakitori*. Tum Tum bought some and began eating happily.

This is just like a baseball game back home, thought the boys.

Suddenly a hush came over the crowded gymnasium. Everyone looked down at a podium on the other side of the gym floor. The grand master, a man dressed in flowing ceremonial robes and a mask, climbed the podium and raised his arms.

The games began. A row of contestants streamed into the arena. Each one was dressed in a martial arts uniform and had a number pinned to his back.

One by one the contestants challenged each other with ninja moves. The best among them was number 7, who let out bloodcurdling screams while defeating the other ninjas.

"Is that what Grandpa wants us to learn?" asked Tum Tum as he gobbled down his *yakitori* stick. "The next level of screaming?"

"Grow up," said Colt.

Rocky was concentrating on the game. Number 7 was winning over and over again. "He's pretty good," said Rocky.

"I could take him," said Colt. He was eager to join the competition himself.

Just then one of the defeated opponents, number 16, joined his mother in the seat behind Colt. He removed his robe and mask and draped it over an empty seat. He had been injured and began tending his ankle with an ice bag.

"I'll be right back," Colt whispered to Rocky as he noticed number 16's robe and mask.

Suddenly number 16 appeared on the gym floor again. Number 7 was surprised to see him. The two opponents faced off. Number 7 twirled twice and leaped a kick toward number 16's shoulder. But number 16 did a double backflip, landed on his feet, and returned with a scissor kick at number 7.

"Hey," said Tum Tum watching from the stands. "That guy's not bad."

"He's kind of wild, though," said Rocky. "Like Colt."

Like *Colt*? Tum Tum and Rocky looked over and saw that Colt was not in his seat. Then they looked at the row behind them. The Japanese boy who was really number 16 was still icing his ankle — but his ninja robe was gone! They realized that Colt had taken the boy's place in the competition!

"Come on," said Tum Tum leaping from his chair. "He's gonna get his brains beat!"

But Rocky pulled his baby brother back to a sitting position. "Stay here," he said. "Maybe this is the lesson Grandpa had in mind."

They looked back down at the face-off. Colt had been holding his own, but all of a sudden number 7 let out a series of swift twirls and jabs. Colt went down and was unable to get back up.

The grand master raised his arms. The face-off was over. All of the ninjas removed their masks.

When number 7's mask came off a long shock of silky black hair shook free. Colt looked up at the victor. He was stunned.

Number 7 was a girl.

"If she's the winner," began Tum Tum, "does that mean we give her this?"

Tum Tum pulled the dagger out from his ninja bag.

"Let's go ask Mr. Big over there," said Rocky.

Rocky and Tum Tum climbed down through the bleachers. When they reached the arena Colt and number 7 had been joined by the grand master. Tum Tum noticed that the grand master didn't wear any shoes. His feet were completely bare.

"Whoa, look at those feet," said Tum Tum, pointing.

"Even in Japan you're a dufus," Colt whispered to Tum Tum.

"Maybe," agreed Tum Tum. "But at least I didn't get beat by a girl!"

Rocky tried to explain to the grand master that he and his brothers had brought the ceremonial dagger all the way from America. But he only knew a few stilted phrases in Japanese.

"Perhaps I can help," offered number 7. "I speak some English."

"Yes!" said Rocky happily. "Tell him we bring this dagger from our grandfather Mori Shintaro."

Rocky pulled the dagger out from his ninja bag

and presented it to the grand master. The grand master said some quick words in Japanese.

"He says he knows everything," number 7 translated. "He spoke with your grandfather from Tokyo. He says the ceremony will wait a few days until Mori Shintaro arrives. We must uphold the tradition."

"What should we do with the dagger?" asked Tum Tum.

"I'll take it!" said number 7. But when she reached for the dagger the grand master stopped her and said something.

Number 7 translated. "The grand master says if your grandfather trusted you with it, so does he."

The grand master bowed to the boys and walked away.

"Colt got beat by a girl," taunted Tum Tum as soon as the grand master had gone.

"I'm still better than *you*," Colt snapped back.

"Shut up, spaz!" said Tum Tum.

"You are a worthy opponent, Spaz," said number 7.

"No," Colt corrected her. "It's Colt. This is Rocky and Tum Tum."

"I am Miyo," said the girl. She led the boys to the sidelines. A woman was waiting there for her. "This is my mother. I would love to hear all about America."

"Where do you stay in Konang?" asked Miyo.

"I don't know," answered Rocky. "We didn't even plan anything."

"Then you will come home with us!" offered Miyo.

"We would be honored," Miyo's mother agreed. "But first we must hurry. We have one more important place to go."

The boys followed Miyo and her mother outside where they all climbed into a car and drove off. After a while they arrived at an open baseball field. A group of Japanese boys were trying out for a baseball team.

The boys smiled. It was just like back home.

Miyo's mother parked the car. The boys followed as she led Miyo to the baseball field. The coach had been expecting them. He gave Miyo a bat. Then Miyo walked up to home plate and began hitting pitch after pitch.

"Every year she is the only girl to try out," Miyo's mother explained as she and the boys watched from the foul line.

Tum Tum noticed an old castle that stood beyond the field.

"Who lives in that castle?" he asked. "The evil umpire?"

"Castle Hikone," said Miyo's mother. "No one lives there. It is very, very old."

Just then Miyo put the bat down, slipped a mitt

on, and ran out into the field. A batter hit a pop fly her way. She ran toward it, beating the other kids there. It landed in her glove, but then slipped out and dropped to the ground.

The coach said something to Miyo. Then Miyo walked off the field and approached the foul line. She looked sad and disheartened.

"He says to come back when I learn to catch," she told her mother.

"Hey, I got an idea," said Rocky. "You teach us ninja, we teach you baseball!"

Everyone smiled at the idea. It was the perfect arrangement.

Over the next few days Miyo and the boys took turns coaching each other.

The first day, they went to the *dojo* and practiced ninja. Miyo showed the boys a special concentration technique. The boys stood in front of each other and "mirrored" each other's movements. She also showed them the proper way to toss five-pointed *shiruken* stars.

The next day, the boys took Miyo out to the baseball field near Castle Hikone. The first thing they taught her was how to chew gum and spit. Then they taught her how to catch by tossing her eggs instead of baseballs. One after one the eggs broke in Miyo's mitt. Finally, she was able to catch an egg without breaking it at all.

On the third day it was ninja training again.

While Colt practiced tossing *shirukens*, Tum Tum found himself bouncing back and forth between two fat sumo wrestlers. The two sumos headed toward Tum Tum at once, but Tum Tum pancaked to the ground. The sumos collided, belly-to-belly with a loud *thump*. Tum Tum crawled between their legs to safety.

Meanwhile, Miyo took Rocky to a small pond with two waterboards across it. She ran across the planks, then signaled for Rocky to do the same. At first Rocky refused. Then he tried to go across slowly.

By the end of the day the boys were following Miyo through the ninja routines exactly. Colt hit the mark with the *shirukens* over and over again. Tum Tum had no trouble outmaneuvering the sumo wrestlers. And Rocky was able to run across the waterboards over the pond.

When the training was over Miyo presented the boys with three new ninja robes. They put them on proudly.

Thanks to their new friend they had achieved the next level of ninja.

12.
Grand Masters
Don't Wear Loafers

Koga swam across his private indoor pool and climbed out. He took a towel from Ishikawa and watched as Glam, Slam, and Vinnie walked along the poolside to join them.

"Where have you been?" asked Koga. He was beginning to grow impatient with his nephew.

"Doing your bidding, oh most respected blood of my blood," replied Glam. "Listen to this."

Glam held out a tape deck and turned it on. Suddenly the sound of shrieking guitars echoed off the walls and ceiling. Koga covered his ears.

"STOP!" he shouted. He reached over and turned off the tape. "Why are you wasting my time?"

Vinnie pulled another tape from his pocket. "Sorry," he apologized. "Wrong tape. No big deal."

Glam took the new tape and put it on. Now Koga listened as Mori told his grandchildren to take the dagger to Konang and present it to the winner of the ninja competition.

"So that is his plan," said Koga. "He returns the dagger to the grand master. Perfection. I will be ready for him. Ishikawa, prepare for our journey."

Ishikawa bowed.

"Hey, what about us?" asked Vinnie. "And our dough?"

"I asked for a dagger," replied Koga. "And you bring me a tape."

"Two tapes," corrected Slam.

"No payment," said Koga flatly. "You have failed me. Ishikawa, take care of them."

Koga turned away, leaving the three bunglers alone with his giant bodyguard. Glam, Slam, and Vinnie backed away, cowering from Ishikawa. Ishikawa reached out and lifted the three failed robbers with one hand.

Then he flung them into the pool.

While Glam, Slam, and Vinnie were trying to keep their heads above water, the three ninjas were enjoying dinner at Miyo's house.

"Rocky," said Tum Tum as he picked his teeth with a fish bone. "Tell Miyo's mother how good this is."

Rocky thought for a moment. *"Tottemo-oushe-*

desu," he said to Miyo's mother. He hoped he had said the right thing.

Miyo's mother nodded graciously. Rocky was relieved.

"Your Japanese is sounding good, Rocky," Miyo told him from across the table. "You should learn something to say to the grand master tomorrow."

"Yeah," said Tum Tum. He was remembering the grand master's bare feet. "Like 'clip your toenails.' "

"I have an idea of what will help," said Miyo. "Come, I will show you."

Miyo led Rocky to her room and showed him a Japanese-English text book.

"This is the book that helped me learn your language," said Miyo.

Rocky squinted at the Japanese letters. "Um . . . I can't really read Japanese," he said. He was too embarrassed to put on his glasses. "You can just teach me a few words."

"No," Miyo insisted. "It's half in English. Don't you see?"

Rocky took a closer look at the book. "Oh yeah," he said. "Could you read it to me. You're better at this."

Miyo sat down next to Rocky. She pointed to some words in the book.

"Go ahead," said Miyo. "Sound it out."

Rocky had no choice. He pulled out his glasses and put them on. To his astonishment, Miyo did not laugh.

" 'Hello. Happy to meet you,' " he read. Then he read the Japanese translation. " *'Konitchiwa, hajema mashtay.'* "

Rocky peeked sideways at Miyo and waited for her reaction. When he looked over he was surprised to see that she was wearing glasses, too.

"Happy to meet you," Miyo said shyly in English.

Rocky and Miyo looked at each other. Rocky moved his hand closer to Miyo's. At that moment they knew that they liked each other very much.

The next morning at sunrise, Miyo and the boys returned to the *dojo*. The grand master had agreed to continue to train the grandchildren of Mori Shintaro. The boys carried their new robes in their ninja bags. In Tum Tum's bag was the dagger.

While the boys went into the *dojo*, Miyo snuck around and found a low window to peek into so she could watch. The boys found the grand master in the main ceremonial room of the *dojo*. He was dressed in his ceremonial robe and his face was covered with a ninja mask. Surrounding him were three *yakuza* warriors.

The boys bowed before the grand master.

"So you are the grandsons of Mori Shintaro," said the grand master.

Tum Tum was surprised. "Hey, how come you didn't speak English to us at the tournament?" he asked the grand master.

"In front of other people?" returned the grand master. "They would not understand us. It would be rude. It is clear you have much to learn about Japanese customs."

"We are here to learn, sir," said Rocky.

"But, first," said the grand master. "Do you have the dagger that your grandfather gave you?"

"I thought you wanted to wait until he arrived," said Colt.

"I changed my mind," the grand master said flatly. "I want it now."

Tum Tum shrugged, bent down, and rummaged through his ninja bag for the dagger. But as he bent down he noticed that the grand master wasn't barefoot anymore. He was wearing an expensive pair of tassled loafers.

Just then one of the *yakuza* guards went to the window and drew the curtains closed. Miyo, who had been watching through the window, could no longer see into the room. She entered the *dojo* through a side door. But as soon as she did, she heard a rattling noise coming from behind a closed door.

Miyo cautiously approached the closed door and

opened it. Inside was an old man, tied up, his hands taped and his mouth gagged. Miyo rushed to the old man and ungagged him. The man quickly told Miyo that he was the real grand master. He had been preparing his ninja lessons when he was abducted by Koga, an old student of his. Koga had taken his robes and, at that very moment, was posing as the grand master in order to get the dagger from Mori Shintaro's grandchildren.

Miyo rushed out and raced toward the *dojo* ceremonial room. She knew she had only a few seconds to save her new American friends.

13.
A Call Home

"NO! HE'S A FAKE!" shouted Miyo. Everyone turned. Miyo was standing at an opened doorway.

Tum Tum reacted quickly. He pulled the dagger away from Koga's waiting hands and stuffed it back into his ninja bag.

"Scramble!" yelled Tum Tum. He and his brothers scattered across the room.

"After them!" ordered Koga. His three *yakuza* bodyguards chased after the three boys.

Rocky, Colt, and Tum Tum joined Miyo and ran through the open door. They found themselves in a room filled with all kinds of ninja supplies and costumes. They quickly looked for places to hide.

When the three *yakuzas* entered the supply room they stopped with caution. The room looked empty.

Suddenly Miyo, Rocky, and Colt leaped out from behind a row of *samurai* costumes. Rocky and Colt threw their ninja bags at the *yakuzas*. The *yakuzas* stumbled and fell forward, right onto their faces.

At the same time, Tum Tum jumped out of a large wooden storage chest. He reached inside his ninja bag and pulled out a handful of jelly beans.

The *yakuzas* reached for their swords. But one of them yanked out his cellular phone by mistake.

"What are you going to do?" Colt said with a taunting laugh. "*Talk* us to death?"

Realizing his mistake the *yakuza* pulled out his sword. Now all three *yakuzas* stepped toward the defenseless kids, their swords flailing.

Soon Miyo, Colt, and Rocky were backed up against a wall. Luckily, some *bo* sticks were hanging on the wall. The three kids grabbed the *bo* sticks and faced the *yakuzas*. Now the odds were evened. The kids warded off the blows from the *yakuzas'* swords and pushed the fight back into the center of the room.

In the meantime, Tum Tum had climbed the rafters of the room. He leaped from beam to beam and began bombarding the *yakuzas* below with jelly bean missiles.

Just then his beeper went off. He looked at his watch. It was two o'clock back in the States. That meant that his mother was expecting him to call home.

"Rocky, give me the phone!" called Tum Tum.

Rocky warded off a blow from the *yakuza* with the cellular phone. Then he reached over and grabbed the phone from the *yakuza's* robe. He tossed it up to Tum Tum. Perching himself on one of the beams, Tum Tum dialed.

"Hi, Mom!' said Tum Tum when Jessica answered. "It's me!"

"It's about time," said Jessica. "You're five minutes late."

Tum Tum looked down from the rafters. "Well, I'm kind of hung up right now," he quipped.

"What's going on there?" asked Jessica.

"Oh, not much," said Tum Tum as he lobbed a few more jellybeans at the *yakuzas* below. "Yeah, they're here. Hey, Colt! Mom wants to talk to you!"

Tum Tum tossed the phone down to his brother who was still blocking sword blows with his *bo* stick.

"Hi, Mom! Oh, hi, Dad!" Colt said into the receiver as he kept fighting.

"Well, this time you've really done it, haven't you?" said Sam who had taken the phone from his wife. "I thought we'd discussed this. I thought there was going to be no more ninja for a while."

Colt pushed the *yakuza's* sword aside with his *bo* stick and then landed a sharp kick to his hip.

"We're not doing, ninja, Dad," insisted Colt breathlessly. "We're just — seeing the sights. Meeting the people."

"When you get home," warned Sam, "we're going to have a long talk about responsibility. A *long* talk."

Colt bopped the *yakuza* on the head with his stick.

"Fine," he replied to his father. "I'll set aside a month. No, I'm not being sarcastic. Rocky wants to talk to you. Bye, Dad."

Colt passed the phone to Rocky who, at that moment, was locked with a *yakuza's* sword.

"Hi, Dad," said Rocky. "The noise? Oh, it's TV! Some kung fu movie. Tum Tum, turn it down!"

Rocky grabbed a nearby rope and, swinging a big loop, knocked the *yakuza* to the ground. SLAM! The noise quieted down.

"No, grandpa's off fishing with his friends," Rocky told his father. Just then another *yakuza* charged him with a sword. Rocky raised his *bo* stick for protection. Then he took the phone and smacked the *yakuza* across the face with it.

The *yakuza* screamed.

"Gotta go," Rocky said into the phone. "Bye." Then he hung up and shoved the phone into the *yakuza's* open mouth.

Rocky, Colt, and Miyo ran out of the room. The *yakuzas* chased close behind and followed the children up a stairway that led to an attic.

The kids crouched inside the attic and scurried along its narrow crawl space. Then they turned and faced the attic opening. A *yakuza's* head popped through. KICK! Colt aimed his foot at the head. The head disappeared through the opening.

The kids scurried to the next opening and peered down. The *yakuzas* were climbing toward them. Rocky and Colt jumped the *yakuzas*, forcing them back through the opening and down to the ground.

"Follow me," said Miyo. "There's a secret passageway to outside." The boys followed Miyo. They climbed down some steps until they reached a door. Miyo kicked the door open. Beyond it was fresh air, the outside.

The kids stepped through the door, but suddenly stopped dead in their tracks.

Waiting for them on the *dojo* lawn was Koga, Ishikawa, and an army of fifteen *yakuzas*.

And there seemed to be no visible means of escape.

14.
Nurses for a Day

Rocky, Colt, Tum Tum, and Miyo were blind-folded and taken for a long drive. When the blindfolds were removed they found themselves in an enormous gymnasium. Twenty ninjas were performing exercise drills. Another twenty were practicing with bows and arrows.

"Let me go!" shouted Tum Tum. He was kicking and screaming at Ishikawa, who was carrying him by his waist. "Let me go, you big ape!"

Ishikawa led the kids down some stairs and into a dungeon cell. It was a dark, dank place with high ceilings. Ishikawa put Tum Tum down, took their ninja bags, and left the cell, locking the door behind him. The kids were prisoners.

"I knew this was a bad idea," said Tum Tum. "Coming to Japan."

"What?" said Colt with astonishment. "You were the one who voted to come in the first place."

"I just wish I was home," said Tum Tum sadly.

"I want to see Mom and Dad. I want to be in my own house and have a real cheeseburger with real cheese."

"I knew this would get around to food," groaned Colt.

Tum Tum pulled out a crumpled photo of his parents from his pocket. It was the one he had taken with him just before leaving his house. Rocky and Colt looked at it sadly. Then Rocky turned to his brothers.

"What is a ninja?" he asked with determination.

"Stop it," said Tum Tum. "You're not Grandpa."

"What is a ninja?" insisted Rocky. "A body — "

"A spirit — " added Colt.

"A mind — " offered Miyo.

Rocky faced Tum Tum. "Tum Tum?" he asked pointedly.

Tum Tum forced the tears back into his eyes. "A heart," he said softly. Then he put the photograph back into his pocket.

Three floors above the kids' heads, Koga stood in his office. He was standing in front of a glass case. In the case was the sword he had stolen from the Japan Museum of History. Next to it was the dagger he had taken from Tum Tum's ninja bag.

Finally, after so many years, both were in his possession.

But it still was not enough.

Koga stormed downstairs to the gym. He marched past the rows of training ninjas to a far corner of the room. There, tied by the feet and hanging upside down, were Glam, Slam, and Vinnie.

"I will give you one more chance," Koga told his nephew. "I have the dagger and the *samurai* sword, but they tell me nothing. Only one man knows their secret. That man is Mori Shintaro. Are you capable of kidnapping an old man? A *hospitalized* old man?"

Glam was so excited he twirled around and around. "If you let us down, Uncle," he started, "I have a marvelous idea!"

As soon as Koga released them, Glam, Slam, and Vinnie dressed up in nurses' uniforms and snuck back into Tokyo General Hospital. With all the lipstick and makeup they were wearing they were able to go about completely unnoticed.

It wasn't long before they spotted Mori rolling by in a wheelchair. He was heading toward his room.

"That was him!" said Slam.

The three hoods approached Mori.

"Uh, sir," said Vinnie in a high-pitched "nurse" voice. "Would you mind coming with us?"

"I already had my physical therapy today," Mori told the "nurses."

Vinnie grabbed the handles of Mori's wheelchair. "This is more in the way of — " he began.

" — discharging you from the hospital!" finished Glam.

The three hoods rolled Mori into an elevator. As soon as the elevator doors closed Slam took out a syringe and vial from his pocket. One shot and Mori would be unconscious.

But when the elevator jolted and began to move Glam was thrown forward. His cap fell off and his white hair came spilling out.

"You!" exclaimed Mori as soon as he recognized Glam.

Suddenly the elevator door opened on the next floor. Mori spun his wheelchair, knocked down the metalheads, and escaped out of the elevator and down the hallway.

Glam, Slam, and Vinnie chased after him.

Mori turned down another corridor, passing some orderlies who were pushing a gurney. Glam, Slam, and Vinnie also turned the corner, only they collided with the gurney. Slam slid under it, while Glam and Vinnie were thrown over it and down the hallway.

Glam, Vinnie, and Slam slid down the waxy floor of the hospital corridor. They were going so fast they almost overtook Mori.

But as Mori turned down yet another corridor, Glam, Slam, and Vinnie continued sliding straight ahead until they crashed into a row of bedpans.

CLANG! CRASH! The metalheads were showered with metal bowls.

Meanwhile, Mori turned another corner. Within no time, the three grungers were chasing him again. Mori glanced back as he rolled down the corridor in his wheelchair. But when he looked forward he saw that he was about to collide with a nurse holding a washbasin.

Thinking quickly, Mori kicked the washbasin out of the nurse's hands in such a way that it flew behind him and landed right in the path of his scruffy pursuers.

Glam, Slam, and Vinnie hit the pan and tumbled over each other in a heap.

Mori raced down a hallway. Glam, Slam, and Vinnie had picked themselves up. Now they were right behind him and gaining fast.

Suddenly, a gurney swung out from nowhere, knocking the three followers off their feet. From behind the gurney leaped Nurse Hino.

"KIYEE!" Nurse Hino screamed, ninja-style. "You're on the wrong floor, *girls*!"

Glam, Slam, and Vinnie stumbled back to their feet. Nurse Hino pushed the gurney at them. Then Mori joined in with a few well-placed kicks from his wheelchair. As soon as the three bumbling kidnappers were piled up on the gurney, Nurse Hino twirled it around and sent it rolling down the corridor —

— and right out an open window.

Outside, just under the window, some orderlies were taking three empty gurneys out of an ambulance. When they looked up, they saw the three falling figures of Glam, Slam, and Vinnie. When they looked down, the three figures had landed on the gurneys.

Mori emerged from the hospital just in time to see the orderlies rush their three new patients toward the emergency room.

What Mori didn't see was Ishikawa, Koga's bodyguard, sneak up behind him. Ishikawa put his hand over Mori's mouth and carried him behind the ambulance to Koga's waiting limousine.

15.
Old Enemies

"Why have you brought me here?" asked Mori. "Why?"

He was sitting in a darkened office looking up at Ishikawa. Ishikawa stared at Mori without answering the question. Answering questions was not his job.

Just then the door opened and a man slinked in.

"Leave us," the man told Ishikawa. "I will continue."

Ishikawa obeyed.

"Who are you?" Mori asked the man. He squinted through the darkness.

"Just a boy," replied the man. Then the man pulled out the dagger of Konang and stroked it gently across Mori's cheek. "A boy you once knew in Konang."

The figure stepped into a beam of moonlight

that spilled into the room through the window. Mori immediately recognized the scar on the man's face.

"Koga!" exclaimed Mori with familiarity. "So this is what has become of you. I remember well your greed."

"But you must remember more, old friend," Koga said sarcastically. "I have the sword. I have your dagger. But the cave of gold. Where is it?"

"Those were just stories," replied Mori. "Stories to entertain little boys."

Koga dug the point of the dagger deeper against Mori's cheek. "Entertain this little boy," he said threateningly. "Or would you like a souvenir like the one you gave me?"

"I remember nothing about the cave," said Mori.

"Then let me help you," said Koga.

Koga called Ishikawa back into the room and told him to take Mori to the dungeon. Once there Koga showed Mori a barred window in the dungeon cell door.

Mori's heart sank. There, inside the dungeon room, were his grandchildren.

"Boys!" called Mori. "How are you doing?"

The boys ran to the door, thrilled at seeing their grandfather.

"We're okay, Grandpa," said Rocky.

"What about you, Grandpa?" asked Colt. "They're not hurting you, are they?"

"Get us out, Grandpa! Please?" It was Tum Tum.

"I'll do my best," said Mori. Then he noticed Miyo, standing further inside the cell. "Who is that with you?"

"Rocky's girlfriend," said Tum Tum with a giggle.

"She's not!" insisted Rocky. Then he caught Miyo's disappointed look. "Well . . . I mean — "

Mori glared at Koga in disbelief. Only a monster would use children in this fashion.

"Don't worry," Mori told the kids. "I will get you out. Remember: four strands of rope!"

Just then Ishikawa slapped Mori on the back and pushed his face into the bars on the door.

"The cave," insisted Koga. "Where is the cave?

Mori searched his memory for the answer. "According to the legend," he began, "the cave is beneath Castle Hikone. The sword and the dagger are the keys. Now let my grandchildren go."

Koga nodded to Ishikawa. Ishikawa pulled Mori off the bars.

"You have somewhere else to go first," Koga told his prisoner. "Castle Hikone."

Ishikawa hustled Mori down the hallway, away from the children. Before he followed, Koga turned to one of the guards that stood at the cell door.

"Eliminate the children after I've reached the treasure," he commanded. The guard nodded and watched as Koga walked down the hall and out of the dungeon.

Rocky and Colt looked all around the cell. They needed a way out.

"A ninja must be able to use everything around him to his advantage," said Colt.

"But there's nothing we can use," said Tum Tum.

Colt reached into his pocket and pulled out a *pachinko* ball which he had taken from the game arcade at the train station.

"I still have a *pachinko* ball," he said.

"I don't even have my jelly beans anymore," said Tum Tum. "Forget it. There's no way to escape."

Rocky looked up and saw some pipes that led to the ceiling. An idea formed in his head.

"We don't have to escape," he said. "We just make it *look* like we did."

A few minutes later the guard could hear the kids making lots of noise and talking loudly. He looked into the cell to see what all the racket was about.

Inside he saw that the kids had tied the bed-sheets together into a rope. Rocky and Colt were stuffing the rope through the bars of the window that led to the outside. The guard laughed. The bars were too narrow even for kids to squeeze through. He turned away.

"Okay. Colt," the guard heard Rocky say from inside the cell, "you go first."

"I'm hurrying," he heard Colt reply.

"And I'll go last," came Miyo's voice. "See you down below."

The guard smiled to himself. Then, all of a sudden, it became very quiet in the cell. Curious, the guard looked back in through the bars.

The kids were gone.

The guard panicked. Had the kids gotten away? He knew if they had, then Koga would blame him and probably have him killed.

He unlocked the cell door and went inside. There was no sign of the kids. He ran to the window and looked out. Still no sign.

Then the guard heard a sound come from above. He looked up just in time to see the four kids drop on him from the ceiling pipes.

Colt knocked him to the ground. Then Miyo caught him on the rebound with another kick. As the guard fell back, Rocky was ready with a chop into his back. Tum Tum added the final blow that sent the guard falling unconscious onto the bed.

Colt grabbed the keys from the guard. Then all four kids ran out of the cell and locked the door behind them. Tum Tum looked through the cell door just as the guard was regaining his senses.

"Don't you just hate us?" Tum Tum asked the guard tauntingly.

"Come on!" said Colt as he led the kids out of the dungeon. "We gotta find Grandpa!"

16.
Escape

"They must be on their way to the castle," said Miyo as she and the boys climbed the stairs that led out of the dungeon.

"We have to go to the castle," said Colt.

"I know where it is," said Miyo.

The kids ran down a hallway. Along the way they spotted their ninja bags. They grabbed them and continued on. They burst into a gymnasium that was filled with Koga's ninjas. The ninjas were lined up in rows practicing precision moves with *bo* sticks. When the ninjas saw the kids they moved to surround them.

The kids were easily outnumbered.

"What shall we do?" asked Miyo.

"We should run," suggested Rocky.

"We should hide," offered Colt.

Then Tum Tum stepped forward. "Colt," he shouted. "We should murderlize them!"

The ninja army closed in around the kids. Then

they began to twirl and snap their *bo* sticks in unison.

The kids nodded to each other. Then they exploded from the center of the surrounding ninjas with a series of repeating kicks. The first four ninjas in their path fell to the ground. The kids grabbed the fallen ninjas' *bo* sticks and continued to fight, continually pushing outward from the center of the circle.

Each line of ninjas was pushed back into the line behind. Eventually they all fell like a row of bowling pins.

Wasting no time, Rocky, Colt, Miyo, and Tum Tum climbed over the fallen ninjas and made it out the door.

In the corridor outside the gym the kids found themselves face-to-face with two *kendo* fighters. They turned to run, but saw that another pair of fighters was coming toward them from the other end of the hallway.

The kids tightened their muscles and braced themselves for another battle.

Rocky, Colt, and Miyo formed a defensive circle around Tum Tum. Tum Tum crouched down in the circle and rummaged through his ninja bag.

The four approaching *kendo* fighters formed a circle around the kids.

Rocky, Colt, and Miyo then reached behind them and grabbed something from Tum Tum. One second later they brought their arms back out. Each kid now had a *kendo* stick in hand.

In no time at all the kids lashed out at their attackers, felling them with a series of swift blows. Once again the floor was littered with Koga's men. The kids jumped over them hopscotch-style and made a run for it.

The kids located another door and went through it. They found themselves in an empty gymnasium.

Suddenly the doors to the gym opened. Ninja fighters swarmed in from every side.

"The roof!" shouted Miyo.

The kids backed out through an unguarded door and ran up the stairs to the roof. Once at the top of the steps the kids stopped in their tracks. The door to the roof was being guarded by a huge, fat sumo.

The kids looked behind them. The ninjas from the gym were climbing toward them.

They were trapped!

Thinking quickly, Tum Tum scurried forward and ran between the sumo's legs. The sumo leaned over — further and further — to see where Tum Tum had gone. Tum Tum, from behind, took aim at the sumo's backside and gave it a kick with both his feet.

The sumo lost his footing. Then Colt and Rocky grabbed the sumo and tossed him down the stairwell with a judo flip. The sumo went rolling down the stairs like a huge beach ball and rammed full speed into the pursuing ninjas. They all went tumbling backwards down the stairs.

The kids laughed as they opened the door that led to the roof. They ran out onto the roof and stuck a chunk of wood through the handle to bolt the door tight behind them. But when they turned around they stopped laughing.

There were two more sumos heading right for them.

"Light up their eyes!" shouted Rocky.

"Let's light these fat boys up!" shouted Colt.

The boys leaped forward, feet first, and landed several kicks into the sumos. It was just like when they were practicing with the dummy at Mori's cabin back home. Only the sumos' eyes didn't light up. They shut tight with pain as they fell to the ground.

Miyo ran to the edge of the roof and pointed to the horizon. Way in the distance was Castle Hikone.

"There!" said Miyo. "That's Castle Hikone!"

"How are we gonna get there?" asked Tum Tum.

Miyo looked around the roof. At the far end of the roof was a set of bat-winged gliders, the same kind Koga had used to escape from the roof of the Japan Museum of History with the stolen sword of Konang.

"On the wings of eagles," said Miyo. She led the boys to the gliders. She and Rocky strapped themselves into one.

"Listen," Tum Tum said hesitantly while Colt climbed into the second glider. "I don't think I can do this."

"Oh, grow up," said Colt.

"This has nothing to do with growing up," insisted Tum Tum. "I just don't think I can — "

Just then the chunk of wood that had been used to bolt the roof door broke in half. The door swung open and Koga's ninjas spilled out onto the roof.

Tum Tum quickly strapped himself in behind Colt on the glider. Then all four kids ran at full speed to the edge of the roof. Tum Tum kept his eyes shut.

"JUMMMMPPP!!!" shouted Miyo.

On her command the kids leaped off the side of the roof. Tum Tum screamed and squeezed his eyes tighter expecting to hit the ground at any moment. But instead of hurtling downward, the gliders took the children higher into the sky and away from the roof of Koga's *dojo*.

Even though they were safe in the air, Tum Tum kept screaming.

"Come on," said Colt. "It's just like a roller coaster."

"I *hate* roller coasters!" replied Tum Tum.

Slowly . . . *carefully* . . . Tum Tum opened his

eyes. He glanced back. The ninjas were shaking fists and yelling at them from the rooftop behind them. Tum Tum couldn't help giggling at the sight. Then he turned his eyes forward. Ahead was Castle Hikone. And it was getting closer with each passing cloud.

17.
The Castle

The black limousine pulled up in front of Castle Hikone. Ishikawa and six ninja guards led Mori out. Koga was the last to emerge.

"We have the keys," Koga said to Mori. In his hands were the sword and dagger of Konang. "Now where is the door?"

Mori threw Koga a hard stare. "The legend spoke of an entranceway near the moat," he answered flatly.

Koga searched the thin band of water that surrounded the castle. A few feet beyond the main entrance was a small patch of criss-crossed wooden beams.

"There!" Koga said pointing to the frame. "Try there!"

Koga's men immediately went to work. They took out some hammers and crowbars and broke through the wooden frame.

Behind it was an entrance.

Koga smiled wickedly at Mori. Then he dragged his old enemy inside.

From high in the sky above, Rocky, Miyo, Colt, and Tum Tum could see their grandfather being led into the castle. They angled their gliders downward. Rocky and Miyo landed gently on the ground. They climbed out of their glider and climbed down a stone staircase that led into the castle.

But Colt and Tum Tum missed the ground and landed in a tree. The rustle of their landing caused one of Koga's ninjas to turn away from the secret entrance near the moat. He walked over to the tree and looked up. All he could see was Tum Tum's head falling straight at him, knocking him unconscious to the ground.

Colt jumped out of the tree and Tum Tum got to his feet. Then they followed Rocky and Miyo into the castle.

In the meantime, Koga and Mori walked down a long, dimly lit passageway. On either side of the passageway were decorations of simple Japanese paintings. At the end of the passageway was a stone wall.

A dead end.

"You see," said Mori. "It goes nowhere. Just a wall."

"No!" shouted Koga pounding the wall with his fist. "I will find it!"

Then Koga noticed a thin opening in the wall. There was also a small hole next to it.

Koga reasoned quickly that these holes must be the "keyholes" for which he had been looking. He took out the real sword and dagger of Konang. Then he inserted them into the holes in the wall.

They were a perfect fit!

A second later the wall began to tremble. Then, as if by magic, the wall opened, slowly revealing another stone passageway behind it.

"The gate to my cave of gold!" said Koga with glee.

Koga removed the sword from the wall. Then he and the others moved through the opening and along the new passageway.

Outside the castle, one of Koga's ninjas was standing guard around the moat. He was getting tired of waiting and took out a cigarette. He searched his robes, but couldn't find a match. Just then he looked up. Another guard was approaching him.

"You have a light?" the first guard asked the other in Japanese.

"Ninjas don't smoke, dufus," the other guard replied. The first guard looked at the other with surprise. Under the hood he saw the eyes of a little boy.

Tum Tum! And he was standing on Colt's shoulders!

Suddenly, a foot came out from under Tum Tum's sleeve and sliced the guard in the shoulder. Then another foot came out from below the first and kicked the guard in the knees. The guard staggered backwards and fell into the wet moat.

Rocky and Miyo jumped out from behind a wall and joined the two boys. Then they all crossed the moat and entered the secret passageway to the castle.

By that time Koga, Mori, Ishikawa, and Koga's henchmen had found themselves in a room at the end of the second passageway. It was very dark and they could hardly see a thing.

"Light the room!" Koga ordered. His henchmen dispersed and lit some candles.

Suddenly the inside of the room came to light. It looked like an empty temple. But instead of gold, the room was filled with dusty skulls and bones. It seemed to be a kind of shrine.

"Here are your treasures, Koga," said Mori with a laugh. "Look! An ancient crumbling mine. Nothing but skulls and bones."

"Liar!" yelled Koga. Red-faced, he refused to believe that the cave of gold did not exist. "The cave is in here! I can feel it! The passageway!"

Koga told Ishikawa to stand guard at the head

of a stairway in the corner of the room. Then he led Mori and his henchmen down the stairs.

Rocky, Miyo, Colt, and Tum Tum walked along the first passageway until they found the opened wall with the small holes.

The dagger of Konang was still jutting out of one of the holes.

"Look!" said Colt. "The dagger!"

"Maybe we should leave it here," said Miyo.

"No," said Rocky. "We may need it."

Rocky removed the dagger from the wall. Then the four kids passed through the opening and into the next passageway.

"I don't like the look of this place," quivered Tum Tum.

Suddenly the open wall behind them slid shut. The kids jumped.

"There's a doorway," Rocky said, pointing ahead. "There must be another room."

The kids continued down the passageway. As they walked, they could make out a flickering light. They moved toward the light and soon found themselves in the ancient shrine filled with the skulls and bones.

"What is this place?" asked Rocky.

"It's creepy," said Tum Tum. "That's what it is."

"It's an ancient shrine," said Miyo.

"The candles are all lit," noticed Colt. "Grandpa must already be in here."

The four kids stepped further into the room. Suddenly a huge shadow loomed over them. The kids turned and screamed.

Before them was Ishikawa. And a menacing grin was stretched across his face.

18.
Ninjas vs.
Ninja-Nuity

Ishikawa stood in front of the kids in the shrine room. He was as big as a wall.

The kids dropped their ninja bags and crouched into fighting position. All at once, they let out a ninja shriek and plowed into Ishikawa.

But the kids bounced off the giant bodyguard like peas that had been shot at a blackboard. Ishikawa stood unflinching.

Thinking quickly, Rocky and Colt hoisted Tum Tum up onto Ishikawa's shoulders. Ishikawa spun around, but finally grabbed Tum Tum and tossed him back to the ground — right on top of the other kids.

Ishikawa laughed loudly and boisterously.

"Huddle!" shouted Rocky. The kids grouped together. They quickly formed a plan and dispersed.

Rocky, Colt, and Tum Tum hid behind an open door. Miyo stood right in front of Ishikawa.

"You're a stupid hippo!" Miyo taunted Ishikawa

in Japanese. "A stupid clown. And your mother's belly button sticks out."

Miyo's taunts enraged Ishikawa. His face turned red and his nostrils began to flare. He charged at Miyo. But Miyo swiftly stepped aside. Just then Rocky, Colt, and Tum Tum pushed the door closed.

SMACK! Ishikawa hit the door head on. Dazed, Ishikawa fell back, pancake-style, onto the ground. The kids fled from the room and raced down the next flight of stairs.

But at the bottom of the stairs were the rest of Koga's ninja henchmen. The kids turned and ran back up into the shrine. They tried to run out, but were greeted by the first two guards whom they had beaten outside the castle.

They were trapped on either side.

With their swords drawn, the ninja guards closed in on the kids. Colt tackled one of them by the knees. Then, with two or three easy kicks, he knocked him unconscious.

Another ninja chased Miyo across a wooden platform. Without warning, Miyo stopped dead in her tracks. Then she grabbed the running ninja by the belt of his robe and threw him over her and onto the ground.

Tum Tum ran under a scaffold, a ninja chasing close behind. Some ropes were hanging down from the scaffolding. Tum Tum easily maneuvered in and around the ropes, but the ninja became hopelessly entangled in them. Tum Tum grabbed a nearby bucket and clamped it down over the ninja's head.

Rocky was cornered by a ninja. Although he was able to ward off the ninja's blows he could find no opening to knock him out. . . .

Colt was dodging another ninja's sword. The ninja chased him up onto a platform of the scaffolding. Colt looked around for a weapon. Then he lifted one of the planks of the platform and knocked the ninja off the scaffolding. No sooner had he done this than a second ninja came up from behind. Colt ran to a nearby ladder and climbed it. The second ninja followed, but Colt caught him in a headlock between his legs. The second ninja lost his balance and fell to the ground below.

Colt looked over to see that Rocky needed some help fighting a ninja across the room. He grabbed a rope that was attached to a pulley and glided across the room with his legs extended. The force of his kick knocked Rocky's opponent into the wall and down for the count.

Tum Tum and Miyo joined Colt and Rocky. The four of them crossed the room and tried to escape through an opening. But some of the ninjas had recovered and were now blocking the exit with a large stick.

The kids turned around and ran the other way.

Another opening led into a dark tunnel. The kids slid through the opening. The ninjas followed, but their stick was too big and smashed across the opening. WHAM! The ninjas ricocheted off the entrance and tumbled back into the room.

Rocky and Miyo followed Colt and Tum Tum through the tunnel. It was so dark that they couldn't see the long drop that was right ahead of them. Without warning Colt stumbled and fell over the drop.

Luckily, Colt landed on a long chute. It broke his fall and allowed him to slide safely downward. A moment later, Tum Tum, Rocky, and Miyo followed down the chute.

Now all four of them were sliding down through the darkness, uncertain of what dangers awaited them below.

19.
Showdown in the Cave of Gold

Koga had led Mori through the maze of passageways until they came upon a large, dark room. Koga lit a torch. The room became bright with flickering light.

"You're chasing fairy tales," Mori told Koga. "And I'm not going to be buried here for your greed!"

Mori charged at Koga. Koga swung the torch at Mori. As he did so the two men got a good look at the room in which they were standing. The walls themselves were made out of pure, shining gold. There were designs carved all over the walls. A huge golden openmouthed dragon was wrapped around the entire room.

The room was a dazzling sight of golden light.

"A fairy tale?" laughed Koga triumphantly. "Here is your fairy tale!"

Mori was astounded. In his wildest dreams he had never expected that the legends of the cave of gold were true. Now it stood around him as real as day.

"The legend was true," said Mori.

Koga pulled out a gun and pointed it at Mori. "And your job is complete," he said with his finger on the trigger.

Mori fell to his knees. "I beg you, Koga," he pleaded.

Koga laughed. "The great warrior begging for his life," he snickered. "Good-bye, Mori Shintaro."

Just then Mori grabbed Koga's leg and flipped him backwards. Koga dropped the gun. Mori stood up and threw a kick to Koga's head. Koga came back with a ninja punch, but Mori ducked.

"I beat you once, Koga," said Mori.

"That was a long time ago, *grandpa!*" Koga snapped back.

Koga and Mori exchanged several ninja blows. After all these years, the two men were still equally matched. Mori landed a kick to Koga's face. Koga fell back and then lunged for the gun, which was on the floor. Mori dived on top of Koga. The two men struggled for control of the weapon.

"Still greedy, Koga," said Mori as they struggled. "For gold or glory at school — always your weakness! I will win, Koga! Because you are controlled by your greed!"

Suddenly the two men could hear the sound of something sliding from inside the huge golden

dragon. A second later Colt shot out of the dragon's mouth, having plunged down the chute that
was inside of it. He was followed by Tum Tum,
then Rocky, then Miyo. The kids landed right on
Mori. The force of the impact pushed Mori and
Koga apart, and Koga lost his grip on the gun. It
accidentally went off as it fell from his hand.

Suddenly the room began to quake from the
force of the explosion. Dust and rubble started to
fall from above.

"Let's go!" said Mori.

"You mean *scramble*!" said Tum Tum.

The kids rushed to the staircase to get out, just
as the ceiling of the cave of gold began to fall in.

But Koga did not move. He did not want to
leave all those riches.

"If you were a real ninja, you wouldn't care
about the gold," Rocky shouted to him.

Koga hesitated. "You have taught your grandsons well, Mori Shintaro," he said. "Quite honorable."

"You were once honorable, too," Mori reminded
him. "Fifty years ago, Koga, I accidentally
scarred your face. But what happened to your soul
is what I truly regret."

Koga's face grew solemn.

"It's not worth it, Koga," said Mori. "Please
. . . for the sake of those two little boys from long
ago . . . come with us, old friend."

Suddenly some more rubble began to fall from the ceiling. Koga looked at Mori. Then he looked back at the cave of gold. Koga realized that Mori was right. Koga dodged the rubble and raced to Mori as he ran up the stairs and out of the cave.

The group headed back through the maze of passageways that had led them to the cave of gold. They finally reached the stone wall that led to the exit out of the castle. But the wall was shut and fallen debris was piled in front of it.

"Rocky pulled out the dagger and the door slammed behind us," Colt explained to Miyo.

"The dagger!" said Mori. "Rocky! The dagger!"

"No, Grandpa," said Tum Tum. "*I* have the dagger."

Tum Tum stuck his hand into his ninja bag and began searching for the dagger.

"Koga," said Mori. "Help me clear out these rocks."

Koga stepped forward. With a series of powerful blows he kicked the biggest rocks away from the door. Once the area was cleared Mori saw a small crawlspace under the door. It was only big enough for someone very small to slide through.

"Tum Tum," said Mori. "You have to crawl under and use the dagger to open the door."

Suddenly the walls began to shake more violently. Debris was falling from all over. The room was filling with clouds of dust.

Tum Tum quickly crouched down and inched his way under the door. When he was safely on the other side he continued to rummage through his ninja bag in search of the dagger. Finally, he unzipped the secret compartment in the bottom of his bag. There, together with his special stash of cream-filled chocolate cakes, was the dagger.

"I found it!" he exclaimed. Then he pulled the dagger out and slid it into the hole in the wall. The door shuddered and then opened. Mori, Rocky, Colt, Miyo, and Koga spilled through.

Koga looked back toward the cave of gold. In his hand he still held the sword of Konang. He tossed it back into the passageway just as the passageway itself collapsed in a cloud of rubble and dust.

At that moment Koga knew that the cave of gold was now locked forever.

Mori, Koga, and the kids headed down the passageway toward the exit from the castle. Suddenly Tum Tum stumbled. His foot got caught in a wooden stair. He was trapped and could not move.

And only Koga saw him.

Koga stopped. He looked at the helpless Tum Tum. Then he looked at the exit and his way to freedom. He turned back and reached out his hand, pulling Tum Tum free. Then he carried the boy ninja out of the castle to safety.

Outside, the sun was beginning to set as the group emerged from the castle and crossed the moat. Koga's guards were waiting for them. They began running toward Mori and the kids, but Koga ordered them to stop. The guards put down their swords and turned away.

Koga turned to Mori.

"A true ninja is free of all desire," he said gently. "It took me a long time to understand this, Mori Shintaro. From our days in Konang until this moment."

Mori smiled and winked at the kids. "Slow learner," he quipped.

Koga smiled. Then he got into his limousine and drove away.

The kids all gathered around Mori.

"You were brave ninjas," said Mori. "All of you."

Rocky brought Miyo forward. "Grandpa, this is Miyo," he said. "The champion of the *dojo*."

"You?" said Mori with surprise. "A young lady?"

Miyo nodded. Mori held out the dagger of Konang, which he had taken from the wall inside the castle.

"Then I came to give this dagger to you," continued Mori. "As this was presented to me by a ninja master, I pass on the dagger to you. You have achieved the highest ninja level. Mastery of mind — "

" — body — " added Tum Tum.

" — spirit — " added Colt.

" — and heart — " said Rocky affectionately.

Mori handed the dagger to Miyo. "Keep this dagger until the day that you too will present it to a young master," he told her.

With a bow, Miyo accepted the dagger.

"This is better than winning the World Series," said Miyo.

"Too bad we missed our baseball game," said Colt. "But it was really worth it."

"I thought the game wasn't until Sunday," said Mori.

"Today's Friday," said Colt. "It's already tomorrow at home."

Suddenly everyone remembered that Japan time was different than United States time.

"If we can get a flight tonight — " said Rocky.

"One day back," said Mori. "We could make the game!"

"SCRAMBLE!!!" shouted Tum Tum.

And scramble they did. They raced to the nearest telephone and ordered airplane tickets for the flight home.

20.
Ninjas vs. Mustangs

On the day of the baseball play-offs, Sam Douglas realized that his team, the Dragons, was three players short. Those three players were his sons. And they were halfway around the world.

He had no choice. He had to forfeit the game to the Mustangs.

"Ladies and gentlemen," said the announcer. A hush came over the crowded ball park. "I'm sorry to have to relay this to you, but because of a shortage of players, the Dragons have announced — "

"PLAY BALL!!!" came a shout from the crowd.

Everyone's head turned. Rocky, Colt, and Tum Tum leaped over the bench and onto the field. And they were dressed for baseball.

Sam smiled.

"You heard 'em!" said the umpire. "Play ball!"

The three ninjas threw themselves into the game. Colt played shortstop, Tum Tum crouched behind home base as catcher, and Rocky took the pitcher's mound.

Keith of the Mustangs was up first. He took Rocky's pitch easily. The ball flew across the field. Keith ran to first base.

Rocky threw the ball to the next Mustang batter. The batter swung, but missed. At that moment Keith raced toward second base and tried for a steal.

Tum Tum threw the ball down to Colt, who made the tag on Keith. But Keith overslid second. And just as he had done in the game before the Douglas boys left for Japan, he tried to spike Colt.

The umpire called Keith safe at second. Colt's temper flared. He wanted to pummel Keith right then and there. But he had learned too much ninja self-control on his adventure across the world. He calmed down and threw the ball back to Rocky. Then he reached out his hand and helped Keith to his feet.

Throughout the inning the Dragons played better than they ever had before.

"These Dragons look like a different team than the one we saw last week," the announcer said. "They're playing like a well-oiled machine."

Next, the Dragons were up at bat. Number 25 hit the ball low. He ran past first and toward second base. The Mustang second baseman picked

up the ball and tagged the oncoming Dragon hard
— punching him right in the stomach.

Number 25 grabbed his stomach and fell over.
Moments later he was carried off the field and into
the dugout.

Sam quickly looked for a replacement. He
pointed to number 21. Number 21 ran out onto
the field.

By the ninth inning the Dragons were losing
four to two.

The Mustangs were up at bat with two outs. A
Mustangs batter hit the ball into center field.
Number 21 was out there and went chasing after
the ball. The Dragons outfielder reached for the
ball, backwards over the shoulder, and caught it
in the webbing of the mitt.

In the process number 21's cap fell off, revealing
a length of long, black, silky hair.

Number 21 was Miyo!

Rocky, Colt, Tum Tum, and the rest of the
Dragons raced into the outfield and cheered her.

The players then gathered around Sam at the
bench.

"It's the last three outs," said Sam. "Let's get
out there and do our best."

The team started back onto the field.

"Wait, boys," Sam held his three sons back.
"Win or lose, I just wanted to tell you that I'm

very proud of you. You're real sportsmen out there. I told you. You learn about life through baseball."

The three boys looked at each other and groaned.

"With a little bit of ninja thrown in," admitted Sam. "I'm glad to have you home, men."

The boys smiled and criss-crossed their four bats.

Four strands of rope," said Colt.

Sam put his hand on top of the bats. "Four strands of rope," he said.

"Now," began Tum Tum. "LET'S MURDER-LIZE 'EM!"

Tum Tum climbed up to bat. On the first pitch he faked a bunt. Then, at the last second, he hit it over the Mustangs pitcher's head. He ran safely to first.

Rocky stepped up next. He swung at the ball and got a base hit.

Now Rocky was on first and Tum Tum was on second.

Colt came up to bat. The Mustangs pitcher began making "horse" sounds at Colt. Then he threw a couple of pitches that nearly hit Colt.

But Colt stayed in control.

Then another pitch came. Colt focused all his ninja energy on the ball. He watched as it got closer and closer, bigger and bigger.

Then WHACK! He smashed the ball. It flew over the field. It was way above the Mustangs heads. It finally reached the scoreboard above the fence and crashed right through it.

Tum Tum ran to third and around to home. Rocky was right behind, scoring another run. Colt raced around the bases.

The Dragons had won, five to four.

The audience cheered. Jessica and Mori jumped up in their seats. Sam raced onto the field and gathered his victorious team.

After the game, Rocky and Miyo walked hand in hand to the parking lot. Colt and Tum Tum followed close behind, giggling.

"You'll show them when you get back to Konang," Rocky told Miyo. "That's for sure." He was certain she would get on the Japanese baseball team now.

Just then three Mustangs bullies came up to them.

"You won the first round, huh?" said one of the bullies.

"But the game ain't over yet."

One of the bullies pushed Colt. Rocky started in for the bully, but Colt stopped him.

"I can handle it," said Colt. He turned to the bullies. "Tell you what. One on one. Your best guy, and you can pick any one of us to fight against."

"Okay," said one of the Mustangs. He pointed to Miyo. "I pick you. You ruined my home run, girl." In fact, it was his pop fly that Miyo had caught in the outfield.

"Oh, come on," said Tum Yum. "She's just a girl."

"Hey," said the Mustang. "You want to play on a guy's team, you play by guy's rules."

"But she's just visiting," said Tum Tum. "Pick me! I'll fight you!"

But the Mustangs ignored Tum Tum and surrounded Miyo. The boys turned their heads. They couldn't bear to see what was going to happen next.

A second later all they could hear were Miyo's screams.

Her *ninja* screams, that is.

When they turned back, they saw the three Mustangs laid out on the ground, flat on their backs.

They never stood a chance.